FOREST HOLIDAY

Forest Holiday

by

DAVID SEVERN

illustrated by

J. KIDDELL-MONROE

London

John Lane The Bodley Head

FIRST PUBLISHED IN 1946

*This book is produced in
complete conformity with the
authorized economy standards*

Printed in Great Britain by
UNWIN BROTHERS LIMITED, LONDON AND WOKING
for JOHN LANE THE BODLEY HEAD LIMITED
8 Bury Place London WC1

CONTENTS

A*

CHAPTER I

A Hitch in Time

DIANA LONGMORE stared through the window of the little teashop; watching the people in the street outside. Sometimes a car would pass, or a grocer's van, but more often than not the roadway was empty. The country town seemed so much quieter than London! Why, only this morning they had taken a taxi through the crowded streets there; Mummy had seen them off at the station, and they had watched grey acres of houses slide by them as the train gathered speed, carrying them out into the countryside.

She looked across at her brother Derek, sitting on the far side of the round table. He was munching a slice of cake, very dreamily; his head turned away from her. He might have been absorbed in thought—or perhaps he was thinking of nothing at all! They were on their own now, all right, Diana reminded herself, and she wondered if she would ever get used to walking into tea-rooms and ordering just what she wanted.

Outside in the street a few drops of rain were beginning to fall; the sky was overshadowed; the room grew darker as she poured out another cup for her brother and finished off the last triangle of bread and butter, scraping all the raspberry jam that was left in the little bowl. Another April shower, and this one looked as if it had come to stay! The weather was typical. All the way down in the train they had passed from spattering gloom to the strange dazzle of a sun shining from a rift of deep blue sky. The clouds had towered in great mountain chains behind the flick, flick, flick of the telegraph poles and the constant, dizzy rise and dip of the wires, and every now and then the window would be tapped insistently with drops of rain; drops that burst into tiny fragments with the force of the impact, so fast were they travelling.

Diana shifted in her chair and, coming back to the tea-room, felt in her coat pocket for the twentieth time that day. Derek saw her pull out the little brown envelope and unfold the telegram inside. He knew what was written there; had the message by heart and felt no need to look again and reassure himself. But he knew that Diana liked to carry things around with her, to re-read a hundred-and-one times. The wire had arrived at home that morning, before they left for the station.

This was going to be good fun, Derek thought; this chance to join up with Crusoe again for another camping holiday with his caravan. He had already written them a letter from Dalehurst, inviting them down for a week or two, whenever they wanted to come.

I'll expect you when I see you. Derek remembered his words. *I've found a good corner here, the forest is looking grand and I can guarantee that Spring is in the air. Guess whom I've met! None other than our old friend Patch Cooper! So try and make it if you can.*

Then followed instructions as to the journey and a P.S. telling them that he had written to the twins and the Crosbies and hoped they would be able to join him, too. This morning's wire, in answer to their letter, ran—*Good work expecting Titch Michael stop have changed camp find me Royal Oak Crusoe.*

"Lucky we didn't leave before it came," Derek remarked, as Diana folded the telegram and stuffed it into the envelope.

She nodded. "He won't expect us to-day, of course. Our letter said the day after to-morrow. I'm glad we were able to start earlier, though, aren't you?"

Derek agreed. "Besides, he doesn't mind when we come. Just fancy him meeting old Skinflint! I do hope *he'll* still be there."

"So do I!" Diana remembered the little gypsy very vividly indeed. Small and brown and wizened; face as wrinkled as a walnut; eyes as black as the currants in a bun; Patch Skinflint Cooper, with his decrepit old horse and creaking waggon, his harness tied with bootlaces and held together with bits of string—he was a man they were never likely to forget. He was a good friend of theirs. Crusoe owed him his own horse and caravan. And yet, when they first met him with the other gypsies, he had come near to wrecking their plans and spoiling everything. That was when they had been trying to build a cabin for Crusoe.

"Fun seeing Titch and Michael again," said Derek, breaking into her thoughts. "I wonder if the twins will make it."

"I hope so," said Diana, forgetting the gypsy for the moment and thinking of their friends the Crosbies and the Sanville twins, with whom they had spent the holidays last summer. "Doesn't it seem ages since we saw them all?"

Derek took another cake and they were both silent for a while. Two terms at school and the Christmas holidays had intervened since then, although the time had done little to dull their memories. Crusoe, too, as they called their friend Bill Robinson, had been hard at work, writing another book. They had caught only a brief glimpse of him when he called at their house last January, looking, oh, so completely different and much, much smarter in his town clothes. Indeed, they had scarcely recognized him for the same person, and had found themselves quite nervous and tongue-tied in the presence of such a very grown-up stranger!

"Derek! when did you say the bus left?" Diana looked up anxiously. They were to continue their journey by road, for the forest lay only ten miles away from them. They had already spent some time with a map, planning out the final stages of their route.

"Five o'clock," said Derek. "From the square. It's just up the road, no distance, but we mustn't be late."

He stood up, scraping back his chair. Diana watched as he strode across the room and envied him the calm manner with which he tackled the waitress and paid the bill. He was big for twelve—or twelve and a half to be quite accurate. Diana was a little over a year younger. He returned in a moment or two and they struggled with heavy rucksacks and mackintoshes and then clattered across the polished floor between the tables. Two ladies taking tea at the other end of the room watched them pass by outside the window; gazing ahead, very intent and serious; humped under the weight of their luggage. They were much about the same height, both inclined to be slim and very long in the leg; the boy dark-haired; the girl's fair hair cut short around her neck and blown all ways as they met a sudden gust of wind. The rain had ceased, but the sky was as gloomy as before.

Thirty yards up the street Diana stopped abruptly; brushing the hair out of her eyes. She had seen the square, green end of a bus moving away from them up the road; increasing speed relentlessly; the deep voice of the exhaust echoing between the walls of the houses.

"Derek!" she cried. "We're late. We've missed it!" and without knowing quite why, they both started to run. Rucksacks jarred awkwardly; mackintoshes trailed over shoulders and the bus, as if taunting them, gurgled and vanished round the bend ahead. Their pace slowed; breathing deeply, they reached the stop sign, where they paused to consult the timetable fixed to the wall of a house.

"Seven-thirty's next bus," said a man as he passed them; saving them the trouble of any further search.

"Seven-thirty!" Derek repeated in a shocked voice. Why, that meant two and a half hours to wait!

Brother and sister looked at each other and Derek frowned as he met Diana's perplexed stare. This was his fault; taking things too easily, back in the teashop. Really, it was high time he had a wrist-watch of his own.

"We shall be so late," Diana said, breaking the short silence. "Why, it gets dark soon after that, and we've got to find our way across the forest."

Derek slipped the strap from his right shoulder and swung the rucksack off his back. There was a wooden bench below the noticeboard and he turned and, very deliberately, sat down.

"We'll have a look at the map," he decided, and undoing one of the pockets, he pulled out a small booklet. *Guide to the Forest* said the lettering on the front; printed across a photograph of trees. He unfolded the map at the end of the book and bumped heads with Diana as they both bent over.

"Here we are," he said, pointing to a name down at the foot of the sheet. "Railway from London comes along this way, and now we want a bus up the Forest Road towards Dalehurst." His finger moved across the map on

top of the printed red line of their route. "This is all
forest here," he explained. "All this green, and Dalehurst
is right in the middle, where Crusoe was staying when
he first wrote. And the Royal Oak . . ." He paused, his
finger straying out from the road. "Here!" he said at
last, pointing to the tiny letters far out in the green-
shaded woodland. "So we must get off the bus about
three miles short of Dalehurst and take this track to the
right. We should find the way easily enough."

"In the dark?" Diana sounded doubtful.

Derek flicked back through the pages of the little guide
and found the photograph he wanted. They both stared
at the picture of the giant tree and re-read the caption.
*The Royal Oak. The largest tree in the forest. It's girth at
shoulder height is no less than 26 feet.*

"There you are," he said, tapping the page with the
back of his fingers. "Largest tree in the forest. *And*
we know exactly what it looks like. We can't make a
mistake."

"But we've got to find our way." Diana did not sound
at all convinced. "And if it's dark we may never get
there." She gazed up at the sky and sighed deeply.
"Looks like more rain. Oh! I do wish Crusoe had stopped
at Dalehurst. That would have been so much easier."

"Well, he hasn't," said Derek impatiently. "Or he
wouldn't have sent us that telegram. And we're lucky to
have this *Guide*. We might not have known anything
about the Royal Oak."

Diana made no reply. As she sat, staring at nothing,
car passed along the road in front of her and disappeared
round the same corner the bus had taken. She looked
after it without interest. Then, as the idea came to her
she grasped her brother's arm, jumping up in excitement

"Derek! we needn't wait for the next bus. We can hitch-hike!"

No sooner said than done! Rucksacks were slung over their shoulders and off along the road they trudged; not hurrying themselves, keeping over on the left-hand side; alert for the comforting noise of the next car to approach and overtake them.

"We shall save hours," Diana said, half to herself, as she turned to look back across the square. Her eyes were bright. She felt keyed up with expectation. This was the first time either of them had begged a lift, out on the highway, and even Derek was feeling slightly nervous; his right hand, fingers clenched, ready to give the thumb sign as the very next opportunity presented itself.

The roadway continued empty, however, and they trudged slowly on round the bend, meeting only a small, rattly car coming towards them, whose driver greeted them with a broad grin—("I'm sure *he* would have given us a lift," Diana said to Derek, "if only he had been going the other way"). Soon they passed by the outermost houses of the small town and were all alone on the black, wet ribbon of road; walking between the browny-green hedges beneath a sky packed full to bursting with smudgy, rainy-looking clouds. The clip-clop of their footsteps on the hard surface and the dreary swish of the wind blowing across the open fields, were comfortless sounds and they could hear nothing else. Side by side, they marched on; feeling the heavy weight of their rucksacks pressing down on their shoulders and backs.

"We'll get a lift soon, never you worry," Derek braced himself, and as if conjured by his words, the distant drone of a car swelled up behind them. They stopped and turned, staring down the road, and as the black shape grew rapidly between the hedges, Derek stepped out a pace and held up his hand, thumb extended. The high note of the car never faltered. Whoever it was must be driving fast, he thought, even as he waited. Then— *whoom!*—and the great, long car was away down the road ahead and droning into the distance like an angry bumble-bee.

Derek stared after it, his hand still giving the signal. Diana brushed her hair from her face, for the wind of the car's passing had swept them like a momentary hurricane. The clouds drifted lower; curtains of shadowy mist moving quite close above their heads. A few, first drizzling specks of rain began to fall.

"Something else!" called Derek, turning again and looking back. "A lorry!" He was taking no chances this time and took up his stance firmly in the very middle of the road.

With a rattle and squeal of brakes the lorry slowed and came to a standstill. The door of the cab was so high up that Derek could only just reach it, and the catch seemed to have jammed. He tugged hard and at last got the door open.

"Dalehurst?" he panted, and the man sitting inside said something gruffly and jerked his head; motioning them to climb in. Feet on the small iron step, Derek hauled himself up, swung off his rucksack and bent down to help his sister. They collapsed on top of each other in the small seat, tangled up in their luggage and mackintoshes. The door proved impossible for them to shut. The lorry driver stretched across an arm, slammed it with a bang, and releasing clutch and brake, they jerked forward and were off; off and away before they had a chance to draw breath or settle themselves.

As they roared between the hedges; covering with every rough beat of the engine the length of many footsteps, their side of the windscreen became gradually obscured by driving splinters of rain. The drops grew larger and a noise of rattling on the cab roof sounded above the note of the engine. Pressing on each other; sitting awkwardly in cramped positions; Derek and Diana began to glow and feel very cheerful, as travellers do who listen to the beat of the rain from a sheltered place and know that they have escaped a wetting. But the lorry was eating up the distance; swallowing the miles of black road and bringing them closer to Dalehurst. Already a dark fringe of trees bordered the roadway fields; trees that approached on each side and were soon lining the route; shutting away more and more of the feeble daylight. The forest!

The lorry slowed again and Derek peered forward through the white diamonds covering the glass. Dalehurst already? Then they must have overshot the mark! Surely not? A signpost ahead reassured him, but the lorry was turning to the left; the driver pulling the wheel hard round. They should have carried straight on! The road on the map led straight as a die between the town they had left and Dalehurst; Derek was certain of this. They were picking up speed again along the new road; the roar of the engine filled the cab with noise and made conversation almost impossible. Plucking up courage, Derek waited his first opportunity and then asked, as loudly as he dared, "You *are* going to Dalehurst, aren't you?"

The driver nodded, without turning his head, but Derek felt scarcely reassured. The man's face was hard to see; a cloth cap came down almost to his eyes and his features were indistinct in the dim light. He seemed disinclined to talk and it was difficult to go on asking him questions.

But they were wrong! Derek was convinced they were on the wrong road. If the man was really heading for Dalehurst, he must be driving there by a very roundabout way indeed.

A mile farther and the trees retired from the edge of the road and gave place to fields again. Why, they were coming out of the forest, thought Derek, staring forward gloomily. But it was no good stopping the man now, and besides, it would look so silly. He might be making a detour to pick up goods or call at some house or farm.

This seemed more than ever likely, for they were soon rattling into a little village. The lorry swung off the road on to a gravelled parking place and stopped with a jerk. Peering out, Diana, who was nearest the side window, saw the pole and swinging sign of an inn. As he switched off the engine the driver gruffly informed them that they were to stay there—he wouldn't be gone more than a minute. They watched him walk across to the inn, push open a door and disappear. Derek was already fumblng with the flap of his rucksack.

"We're miles out of our way," he said, pulling out the guide, and Diana turned a horrified face.

"We're not going to . . . but Derek he *told* us Dalehurst. You asked him twice."

"Well, we're not going straight there, that's certain. And we want the Forest Road. Here, hold this end," Derek bent close to the map. "Light's poor," he muttered. "Now, we came up this way and—yes, there you are," he cried, almost triumphantly. "I *knew* we shouldn't have turned off to the left. This is where we are now; Littlecombe, the first village along here. We're driving in the opposite direction."

"But, Derek, if he's going to Dalehurst . . ."

"He'll drive all round the place, probably, and bring us in from the North. We don't want the town itself, remember, but a point about three miles south of it, on the Forest Road. The Royal Oak's across on the other side. We're at the opposite end of the forest, now."

"Then we can't possibly get to the Royal Oak to-night," said Diana determinedly. "Let's find somewhere to sleep in Dalehurst." Even as she voiced the idea, she was astonished at herself. Hotels were frightening enough places, staying in them with one's parents! But a desperate situation called for desperate measures.

Derek hesitated before replying, for he was thinking things over and another plan was forming in his mind. A night in Dalehurst was one possibility, that was certain. But he could not bring himself to the idea, although he was not nervous at the prospect, like his sister. No, Derek was thinking of the bill to be settled next morning, and his whole being rebelled against such unnecessary expenditure. Daddy had given them a pound each, and bed and breakfast in Dalehurst would, he knew, knock a very large hole indeed in the sum of their fortunes. As a last resort, perhaps. And Derek bent over the map again, tilting it forward to catch the dregs of grey light from the sky.

"We can get back to the Forest Road another way," he said at last. "And come out much nearer Dalehurst, almost opposite the track we want. Let's try it, Diana! We might get another lift, and at a pinch, we'll sleep the night in Dalehurst, like you said. It's stopped raining."

True enough, the pattering on the cab roof had ceased and everything was still. Derek folded up the map and they both stared across at the dark shape of the inn. One yellow window threw a faint gleam on the rough gravel space outside; lamplight and daylight struggling together for supremacy.

"All right," said Diana. "If you really think . . ."

Derek had already forced the stiff catch of the door. Clumsily they stretched feet down to the iron step and down again to the ground; dragging their rucksacks after them. With a last backward glance at the inn, they set off down the road; breathing more easily as they left the lorry behind them.

"I'm glad he didn't come out." Diana hunched herself, looking up the grey-black, empty street. "I wonder whatever he'll think!"

Derek was not worrying himself about the driver's likely reactions. The tower of Littlecombe church rose ahead of them; solid against the low-flying clouds. On the far side, if he had read the map correctly, they would find a lane down to the right; a small roadway to lead them back towards the forest and Crusoe's camp. They met a couple of villagers, who stared at them curiously as they stumped by, making a great noise with their heavy boots. Then the churchyard wall ran in place of the hedge and a cedar threw massive arms above them.

"Here we are," said Derek quietly, as the wall ended and they turned down a narrow road, sunk between high banks.

"We'll never get a lift this way," said Diana. "We were on a main road, before."

Derek inwardly agreed with her. They were not likely to meet much traffic along this particular lane. And how far were they from the Forest Road? Quite a few miles. And the Royal Oak was another mile or so beyond, again. Derek whistled thoughtfully as they plodded along. Perhaps, after all, they would have done better to stick to the lorry.

"It's raining again, now," said Diana. "Harder than ever."

She did sound gloomy, thought Derek, glancing at her sideways. He must try and keep her spirits up and help her along.

"Last time I said we'd get a lift soon, something came. D'you remember?" he began cheerily.

"And didn't stop," said Diana. "Went by at sixty miles an hour. I remember."

Derek felt slightly dashed. "Well," he continued, trying to make the best of it, "suppose I try again? It may help a bit."

He waited, but there was only a sniff from Diana. He tried to make out her face in the dim light.

"I think something's coming *soon!*" he announced, after the shortest of pauses. His voice sounded really bracing and he felt quite cheered up himself. His stride lengthened and he held his head a good deal higher.

A moment later he had stopped dead in his tracks. "Listen!" he exclaimed, gripping his sister by the arm. "Oh, Di, I really think . . ." He sounded quite incredulous; as if this were just too good to be true! Between dripping hedges and under a blue-grey canopy of heavy cloud, leaking a steady trickle of rain; the dusk filling every nook and cranny with deepening shadow, they stood together, listening intently. And ringing out sharp and clear on the road behind them, coming rapidly nearer, beat the clippety-cloppety rhythm of a trotting horse.

They turned and stared; standing quite still; never taking their eyes from the bend. They did not move even when a pony and tall trap came into view; nor

smile at the sight of the giant umbrella covering the seat
and almost brushing the hedges on either side. Quietly,
they waited. Reins tightened; the clip-clop faltered as
the pony slowed and stopped, and a woman's voice
hailed them; a hearty, comfortable voice from the bundle
up there on the seat, swathed in coats and rugs and
sheltered under the great, round wing of the mighty
umbrella.

Strangely enough, she seemed to be expecting them,
but Derek was too thankful and relieved to realize this.
Someone was offering them a lift; that was enough for
him. And Diana was eager only to climb aboard and let
pony and trap carry them where it would. But as they
prepared to mount the step and sit themselves down
beside her, the driver's excited remarks penetrated
Derek's understanding.

"Why hadn't they waited at Littlecombe?" she demanded again, and rushed on without waiting for an
answer. She had arrived only five minutes late and would
have met the bus if Mr. Crawley hadn't insisted on fixing
the umbrella for her at the last moment. Did they think
they would have to walk the whole way, with their
luggage and all, this showery weather? Hadn't Mr.
Crawley made it clear that she, Mrs. Potts, was going to
meet them? And Cynthia sent her love to them and was
so excited, the little dear, at the thought of their arrival.
"You've never seen your cousin Cynthia, now have you?"
concluded the large woman wrapped in shawls.

Derek gave his sister a helping hand and the trap
swayed on it's springs as they settled themselves on the
narrow seat.

"No," he stammered, with perfect truthfulness. "N-no.
We never have."

CHAPTER 2

Top of the Tower

A LARGE, black cloud—perhaps one of the clouds that Derek and Diana had seen hanging over the train earlier in the afternoon—now filled the sky directly above the forest. Rain was showering down from it; glistening on bare twigs and brown buds and dripping from branch to branch, to fall at last on to the carpet of last year's leaves. In summer the trees would have afforded good shelter, but as early in the year as this the roof of twigs over the Crosbie brother's heads was a leaky one indeed, and Titch hunched his shoulders, growling dismally under his breath. Then, noticing a dead tree thickly covered with ivy, he pushed his bicycle off the path and headed towards it, closely followed by Michael. A moment later they had propped their loaded cycles against the trunk and were standing in the dry; listening to the plip-plop of the rain striking the heavy green leaves above them.

"Only a shower," said Michael, wriggling in between the hard ropes of the ivy stems. He had already made the same remark three times that day.

Titch was fed to the teeth with April weather, and only grunted a reply. One moment the sun was shining and they were boiling hot; the next, down came the rain and on had to go their clumsy waterproof capes again. Rotten for camping out too, with the ground so damp and little dry wood for a fire to be found anywhere. When they had decided to cycle down from Copplestone, they had hoped for a fine spell to help them on their way!

Tent and groundsheet, folded and packed up tight, were fastened behind Titch's saddle. A kettle and a frying-pan hung from the large bundle. Michael's saddle-bag was stuffed to bursting with clothes and provisions and he had tied another package in front of his handle-bars. They had started off yesterday morning, waving good-bye to Jean and their father and, taking things easily, put forty of the sixty miles behind them before evening. Titch, of course, could have covered the whole distance in the time and not felt it. He was in his last year at school and although not brainy enough for the Sixth, had made his mark in the Gym and on the playing-field. In build very like his father, Laurence Crosbie the artist, he was a burly young man; cheerful and good-natured.

Michael, five years younger that Titch, for Jean, their only sister, came between them (the jam in the sandwich, the family sometimes called her!), was fair-haired and slightly built and, according to his big brother, "always fiddling about with paint and pencils." There was no doubt that he had inherited something of his father's gifts, and spent as much time in the Art Room as Titch in the Gym. He was quiet and rather shy and had made few friends, while his brother knew everyone and was universally popular. But in spite of these differences, and the gap in their ages, Titch and Michael had always got on well together. Michael would have followed his brother anywhere, and he knew that at heart Titch respected his "scribblings," however much he might joke and tease him about them.

The Crosbie family had met Crusoe and his friends the summer before and had joined them for a tour with a circus and, finally, a holiday up in the hills. So when they heard from Crusoe that he was off again this spring in his caravan, camping at Dalehurst, the two boys had at once decided to join forces with him. Last night, on the way down from their home, they had pitched their tent on a common. The ground was very stony and the pegs were difficult to drive in. It came on to rain after dark; the wind buffeted noisily, and they had scarcely dropped off to sleep when the whole side of the little tent was lifted into the air and flapped, wet and rough, across their faces. What a time they had had, fastening the guys down again; the rain soaking them as they struggled in the cold! Michael still shivered at the thought of it! No wonder they woke in the morning stiff and tired and that to-day's April showers depressed them beyond measure.

"We're in the forest, anyway," said Michael, trying to look on the bright side. "I don't expect we're far from Dalehurst now."

Titch grunted again. He had suggested a cross-country ride through the trees as a change from the high-road, but the paths had proved bumpy and knobbled with roots and they had pushed their bicycles for most of the time. He had no idea which was the right direction and was trusting to luck to bring them out on another road, where they might meet someone and inquire the way.

"We'll be able to camp with Crusoe to-night," Michael continued cheerfully. "And it won't matter if it does keep on raining. Rained enough in the hills, didn't it? That's the best of a caravan." He looked up through the dead boughs of the tree; bark scaling off and revealing the wood beneath, smooth and grey as steel. There was a warm glow in the sky; somewhere the sun was pushing through again, low down and near the horizon. "Titch, it's clearing up," he cried. "Don't let's wait any longer!" And the polished ivy leaves shook and dripped on them as they laid hold of their bicycles.

Titch hummed to himself; his face brightening with the sky. Once on the path, he swung his leg across the saddle.

"Look out!" warned Michael. "We'll be skidding on all the wet." But Titch was off, regardless; wobbling and jolting his way along between the trees. He had quite recovered his spirits! Michael, clutching tight hold of the handlebars and concentrating on the track ahead, pedalled cautiously after him through the fine rain.

The path began to climb more steeply and they were soon forced to dismount again. Then a shaft of light sloped between the trunks and spread long strips of gold across the deep brown carpet of withered leaves, now glistening and damp. As they climbed, so the sun gradually sank and turned orange; very large behind the far fringe of woodland. They joined another, well beaten path; plodded round a corner and stopped dead. Michael stared and Titch whistled his surprise. Then they strode forward with sudden, new enthusiasm, to stand at last, craning their necks, beneath a huge wooden erection built in the clearing on the hilltop and rising high above the surrounding trees.

"Just look at that!" was all Michael could say, but Titch had already noticed the steps, mounting in short sections from platform to platform, up to the cabin with a long window right at the very top of the tower.

"Come on," he said, leaning his bicycle against one of the three main uprights. "We'll get a view of the whole forest from up there."

"D'you think we're allowed . . ." Michael began, but

Titch was already climbing the first flight of wooden steps and, once again, there was nothing for Michael to do but to follow. Up through a hole in the planks they went, to stand on platform number one; a triangular-shaped floor built between the three gigantic trunks that soared, tapering and leaning slightly inwards, to the cabin at least five more platforms above them. These uprights were pine trunks; surely the largest and tallest pines that ever grew in England. Down at this level they were each as thick as three telegraph poles and must be eighty feet tall if they were an inch. But Titch was clattering up to the next platform and Michael roused himself and climbed after him.

Standing on the second story, they found they were level with the centres of the trees around. The flimsiest of cross-struts enclosed them; there was no solid barrier, no railing at the edge of the planks. Climbing again, for Titch did not pause for breath, Michael found the steps far too open and exposed for his liking. He was already uncomfortably aware of their height above the ground. As he came through the floor of the third platform he edged very cautiously round and grasped the next flight of steps; holding on tight as he climbed. He tried not to look about him, but there was nothing to hide the view. The tower was the merest open framework. Already the feathery summits of the trees were waving on a level with his head and a breeze ruffled his hair; a breeze that grew stronger, step by step, as he mounted, until, emerging on to platform four he faced into a fresh wind.

He felt a sudden exhilaration. His mind filled with vague thoughts of sailors, hanging like monkeys from the shrouds and cross-trees of tall sailing ships; exposed to the rush of the wind and high, dizzily high above the endless, grey-green rollers. Looking around he could see, over the neighbouring tree tops, the waves of their own ocean; the misty blues and browns of the distant forest rising and falling, clothing all the hills and valleys for miles around. He started to climb again, for his first, slight giddiness had passed. There was nothing near at hand, now, to emphasize their height. They had mounted into another kingdom, and the floor of tree tops hemming them in seemed as solid and secure as the invisible ground beneath.

Titch, a broad grin on his face, was waiting for him on platform five.

"This is all right!" he exclaimed as Michael stood beside him. "I've just heard someone talking in the cabin, so we're not the only ones up here."

They waited for a moment, Michael breathing deeply, and this time they both heard the voice, as the person above them spoke again.

"Sounds as if he's talking on the 'phone," Michael whispered.

Titch was about to laugh at the idea when the voice ceased; followed by the unmistakable click of a replaced receiver. His expression changed. Very quickly, he began to mount the last flight of steps. His head disappeared into the hole in the cabin floor and Michael heard his voice, muffled but polite, as he asked whether he might come in. The answer must have been in the affirmative, for Titch's body and legs began to follow after his head. A moment later Michael joined him, and the Crosbie brothers found themselves in the strangest little room they could have possibly imagined.

The man in the tweed coat, who was stooping down to a large, multicoloured map pinned on the wall,

glanced at them over his shoulder. Then he turned back
and marked something with his pencil. He was pale and
wore horn-rimmed spectacles and seemed very little
interested in his two visitors. When he had finished what
he was doing, he returned to the corner behind them
and sat down on a camp chair by the telephone. The room
was all corners, Michael thought, looking round. Each of
the three walls contained a long, narrow window, making
observation possible in every direction. The man was
talking again on the telephone. What was he saying?
Smoke seen such and such a place; map references and
instructions—why, of course! This was a look-out and
he was keeping watch for fires!

The problem solved, Michael turned to the windows.
And what a view! Why, the hill on which this tower was
built must be one of the highest in the forest. He could
see for miles over the soft carpet of tree tops, rippling in
the wind. Not so far away was an open space; a wide
glade running between low ridges, and he caught the
glint of water; a stream or a chain of ponds. From the
same window he could see a church tower and a few
houses; a mile distant, possibly more. Excited, he called
to Titch. Perhaps they were looking at Dalehurst, he
said. If so, they weren't very far from their destination.

But the man with spectacles, putting down the receiver
and joining in the conversation for the first time, poured
scorn on the idea.

"You can't see Dalehurst from here," he said. "And
if you could, you've got your back to it, as you're standing
now. You're looking at Littlecombe."

Titch and Michael faced round the other way. The
man was right, of course. Looking in this direction they
could see trees, nothing but trees, to the horizon.

"Can you give us any idea how to get there," Titch asked him. "Describe a landmark or two, or . . ."

It appeared that the man with spectacles had lived in Dalehurst all his life, and that nothing was easier. Titch was soon submerged in a flood of directions. Michael, nodding now and then in an intelligent way, left his brother to disentangle the route. There was a roll of bedding on the floor and a detective novel, and they caught his eye. Then a watch was kept by night? Of course, fires didn't stop when it was dark—but to be all alone up here, through the long hours of the very early morning! No, Michael did not envy the man his job. From the floor he glanced out of the window nearest him; glanced again and then stared hard.

"I say!" he called, interrupting the stream of description and explanation, much to Titch's relief. "Do come and look. Isn't that a fire over there?"

Titch and the man with spectacles were beside him in a moment, for sure enough, a small column of smoke was curling up from the corner of the open glade. But, to Michael's disappointment, the sight of it caused no dramatic rush to the map and to the telephone.

"That's a gypsies' fire, that is," said the fire-guard calmly. "Those meadows aren't what you'd call in the forest proper, and there's a camp down in the hollow this time of year."

"Gypsies?" Michael repeated eagerly. Why, hadn't Crusoe said something in his letter about meeting with one of his old Romany friends? Perhaps this was the place! If so, they might find him there. They must certainly visit the camp, even if it did lie in the opposite direction to Dalehurst.

The man with spectacles, who took little interest in

B

gypsies, was talking again. He was telling Titch about
fires he had seen and helped to fight. "I'm a forest
warden," he was saying, and showed them his badge.
"But I got lumbago so bad, see, they put me and another
fellow on this job. We take it turn by turn." He told
them, then, that the spring was much the worst time
for fires.

"What, with all the rain we've been having!"
cried Titch, surprised. "I should have thought the
summer."

The fire-guard shook his head. "Bracken's green and
fresh, then," he explained, "there's nothing to catch
alight. Now, you've got all the dead undergrowth. Like
tinder it is."

Michael was becoming more and more impatient. He
wanted to get down to the ground again and visit the
gypsies, quickly, and find out if they had seen Crusoe and
knew where he was. Already the sky over to the west
was flushed; the clouds massing, rosy and golden and
purple-shadowed. If they didn't hurry they would never
reach Dalehurst before dark.

Eventually, Titch decided it was time they made a
move. Thanking their host, they proceeded backwards
down the steps; leaving the sheltered cabin for the open,
windy skeleton of the tower beneath. They descended
more speedily than they had climbed and the tree tops
reached up and rose around them, shutting away all but
a faint whisper of the gale that rushed by overhead.
Down on the earth again, they felt the air quite stuffy.
Titch bent over his bicycle, grumbling under his
breath.

"This puncture's getting worse," he said. "Not so jolly
slow, now. I shall have to do something about it."

"Not this minute!" said Michael anxiously. "Pump it up hard and wait till we get to Dalehurst."

Titch regarded the tyre; hand cupped under his chin. "I suppose it can wait," he decided. Then, glancing round, he saw Michael, foot on pedal, prepared to push off down the track to the left. "Not *that* way, you chump. Didn't you hear what the fellow said?"

"But we're going to the camp first."

"Camp?" Titch repeated, surprised. "Oh, you mean the gypsies! D'you think . . ."

"Crusoe might be there, Titch. We must," Michael insisted.

Titch reached for the pump. "Carry on, then," he said, with a gesture of his hand. "I'll follow in half a minute."

Michael needed no second bidding, and shot off down the slope; rattling and bumping along the track between the thickets and withered bracken and small holly trees. This was the direction all right, and as soon as he came out into the open meadows, he would see where he was. Keep going down-hill; that was the safe way to reach the stream in the valley bottom.

The path twisted, forked, bent between large trees; crossed larger rides at right-angles. This glade was farther away than he had bargained for. The way up again would be a hard pull and the direction not so easy to find. He should have thought of that before. But going down-hill as fast as this; shaken to bits and concentrating hard, Michael could not spare the time to worry. He hoped Titch would be able to follow in his tracks—and dashed on.

At last the trees thinned; he saw a stretch of green ahead, and his frantic pace slowed as the slope eased off.

The track bent round and ran by the side of the open
meadowland; a narrow belt of coppice and undergrowth
between. Michael could wait no longer, but propped
his bicycle against a sapling and plunged into the thicket.
He struggled over a ditch and a wire fence, and with a
jump landed outside the forest, both feet on the short
grass of the meadow. Quickly he looked to the left and
right; he had no idea how far he had come. For a moment
he was disappointed and saw nothing; then his spirits
rose. There, behind a small promontory of trees jutting
out into the grass; surely he was not mistaken? That was,
that *must* be, the painted side of a caravan!

As he drew nearer, walking along by the meadow's
edge close to the border of trees, Michael decided to
approach cautiously and spy out the land ahead. Crusoe,
Derek, Diana and the twins had talked a lot about the
gypsies they had met last summer, but that was before
he knew them and this was to be his first encounter with
the Romany folk. After all, as a stranger, it was best not
to walk into the camp unannounced. So Michael, stepping
quietly, made his slow way round; hoping he would see
one of the gypsy children and be able to find out about
Crusoe without creating any sort of disturbance. As he
peered through the tree trunks, he saw that he was now
quite close to the waggon he had glimpsed on coming
out of the forest. He looked again, for the colours, red
and green, struck a familiar note. Gaining courage
he crept round the promontory and stood gazing at
the solitary caravan, standing in the sheltered bay
behind.

Nothing stirred. Everything was quite still; no wreath
of smoke curled from the black chimney; the shafts lay
on the ground and no horse clomped a hoof and nibbled

the grass nearby. The forest, thrusting an arm of oaks and hazels out into the meadow, curved round behind and formed an ideal camping-place. There was no other waggon in sight. They were not so far from Dalehurst here; this might be the place he had chosen. But *was* this Crusoe's caravan?

The colours were the same and the shape was, surely, identical. Michael thought back to the summer holidays; such ages away. If he could only remember one outstanding detail, to check up with his memory. He stepped closer. There was no-one about; the waggon was obviously deserted. He stared up at the porch, the carving; looked at the steps. One glance inside would settle matters, but for the life of him he could not make up his mind to open the door. He felt there was something odd, something different about this solitary waggon. What exactly was wrong? He walked round; stopped, and looked again. Of course! Where were all the usual signs of a camp? The litter and rubbish and stuff that usually accumulated round a waggon? Even the grass was not trampled; why, the caravan might have been left here, to-day, for the first time.

Michael pulled himself together. He went straight to the steps, but even as he climbed, something told him that this was a strange waggon. He turned the handle very gently, half expecting to find the door locked, but the catch opened and he peered inside. One glance was enough, and confirmed his suspicions. Everything was completely different. He noticed a set of harness lying on the floor and hesitated, about to retreat. At that very moment he heard the sound of voices. The gypsies were coming! They must be quite close! They might have seen him at the waggon door! In sudden panic, afraid of being

caught, he turned, missed his footing, and slithered to the
ground. When he tried to run, a stab of pain slowed his
pace to a hobble. Gasping, he put his hand to his ankle
and then, as best he could, limped to the border of the
forest and crawled between the trees.

CHAPTER 3

Romany Rai

MICHAEL, when he first reached the cover of the forest, hardly dared to look out, so certain was he that the gypsies had seen him. At last, furtively, he peeped through the interlacing twigs and branches and saw that a large body of men and women, dressed soberly in black, but with the dark skins and flashing eyes of their race, were walking across the meadow towards the caravan. As they drew nearer—there must have been twenty of them, talking together quietly or staring at the ground—he forgot his fears. They were obviously not concerned with him and could not have seen him on the waggon steps. The manner of their approach, their strange clothes, puzzled him as he squatted in the dead bracken and watched them come. They were not *his* idea of gypsies. Only their brown skins and unmistakable features were true to type. Although to-day was a weekday, they were all as smart as if dressed in their Sunday best; the men in black suits of a curious cut and the women in old-fashioned black gowns and hats. Their shawls alone added a few spots of colour to the scene. Where was the ragged, noisy, happy-go-lucky crew of ne'er-do-wells that Crusoe and the others had so often enjoyed talking about?

Still nursing his ankle, Michael saw them group themselves around the caravan. Two of the men climbed the steps and disappeared inside, and as he watched, began to hand out piles of crockery and pots and pans; pictures and mirrors and mantelpiece ornaments. Willing hands seized them and made a pile on the grass. Fenders appeared, and fire-tongs, and poker . . . and suddenly, one of the gypsy women seized this implement and without a moment's hesitation began to wield it, with devastating effect, among the heap of breakables!

Crash! Smash! Michael's eyes opened wide at each blow and he stared out from his hiding place in complete amazement. Nobody interfered or tried to stop her; the others all stood around, watching, as if it were the most natural thing in the world. Now a second woman had picked up a weapon of some sort and was pounding at the heap; pounding the glass and china into dust and fragments. Why, they were trying to beat the very kettles and saucepans flat!

Michael's fingers itched; he longed to grasp a poker and join in the fun himself. Never before had he seen grown-ups indulging in such an orgy; only gypsies would be capable of doing anything like this! And yet, he thought, as he watched them, they didn't seem to be enjoying themselves. They were all so quiet and undemonstrative; as if it were all entirely a matter of course. He would have had them shout and yell and dance round the pile of crockery, brandishing their weapons. As it was, they were much too methodical and business-like about the whole thing.

So taken up was he with this wholesale breakage that he had failed to notice what was happening over by the caravan. The crowd, leaving the piles of household goods, had moved across to the waggon, and one of the men, standing on the top step, started to shower the contents of a large can through the open doorway. Michael saw this happen and thought vaguely of water. But almost at once, with a sudden *pouf*, a sheet of fire hid the entrance and the gypsy leapt down, shielding his face with his arm. Michael heard a low murmur grow rapidly louder and swell to a fierce roar as the bedding and curtains burst into flame.

Another gypsy, picking up the battered remains of a saucepan, hurled it through the waggon window. Following the crash of broken glass, tongues of fire licked out through the hole and curled up and over the roof; the air shimmered with the heat and the trees behind bobbed and swayed indistinctly. Encouraged by the through-draught, the flames roared louder and gripped the whole wooden framework of the caravan. The stench of scorching paint drifted over the meadow, and oily clouds of smoke billowed up. Michael could scarcely believe his eyes. Smashing piles of crockery was one thing, but to set fire to a waggon, in perfect condition and fully furnished; to make a bonfire of a caravan—that was quite another. What was it all about, anyway? What were they doing it for? There was no sense in it, as far as he could see, unless they were getting their own back on somebody. Michael shivered at the thought. What a revenge! There would be something to pay for this, afterwards, was all he could keep repeating, as if to balance things in his mind. And the crowd of gypsy men and women, driven back by the heat and forming a wide circle round the burning waggon, gazed on their handiwork with calm faces; expressing neither satisfaction at what they had done, nor fear of the consequences.

Titch, spurting to catch up with his brother, pedalled furiously down a steep track towards the hidden clearing. His tyres, now tight and hard, bumped and bucketed him about all over the place; he brushed the undergrowth

B*

now on this side, now on that, and kept his balance only
by a miracle. Utterly unprepared for an emergency, he
charged full tilt round a sudden turn. The next moment,
brakes locked, he had slithered sideways off the track, and
with a jangle of pots and pans, crashed through a hazel
bush and sprawled his length on the damp brown floor
of leaves.

The cause of the disaster; a tall, silver-haired old
gentleman, who had been picking his careful way down
the muddy path, jumped half round, looked wildly about
him and then hopped to the side of the track, as if
expecting a dozen more cyclists to come hurtling in
Titch's wake. The silence evidently reassured him, for
moving his long legs like a stork and placing his neat,
brown shoes with great care only in the driest places, he
climbed to the scene of the accident and inquired whether
anyone was hurt.

Titch, extricating himself from under the back wheel
of his bicycle, had little breath to spare for a reply. He
began to brush away the leaves that clung to his clothes,
and greatly to his relief, found himself whole and
unhurt.

"My fault," he said, eyeing the neatly dressed stranger
a little askance. "I never expected to meet anybody else
down here. You don't happen to have seen my brother,
do you? Has he passed this way?"

The old gentleman shook his head. He, in his turn,
eyed Titch severely; as if he were not at all accustomed
to meet with reckless young men on bicycles, riding to
the common danger along the forest paths. "Most certainly not," he said. "Was he also . . ." And he pointed
his walking-stick distastefully at one of the mud-caked
tyres.

"Where *can* he have got to?" Titch exclaimed. "Yes, we're both cycling. He wanted to find the clearing, the place where the gypsies are camped. That is down at the bottom here, isn't it?"

The old gentleman looked at him with new interest. "Carry straight on," he said. "May I ask if you and your brother are interested . . ."

"It's not so much that, but a friend of ours may be camping with them," Titch hastened to explain. "I expect I'll meet him there. Thank you very much." And he hauled up his bicycle, disentangling broken twigs from among the spokes.

"I doubt if you'll be able to ride much further," said the old gentleman. "The path drops very steeply after this. As a matter of fact, I was going that way myself, and if you'd care to come along—at a more sober pace," he added with a slight smile, "I might be able to help you. I scarcely think it would be advisable for you to visit the camp just at present. Indeed, I rather hope your brother has not succeeded in finding his way there."

Titch stared at him blankly, without grasping the drift of his remarks. Then he pushed his bicycle out on the path and followed behind his newly-found guide, who was already performing an uncertain tight-rope act from clod to clod, waving his stick in the air and then plunging it deep into the mud.

This old man, in his neat, heather-coloured tweed suit and cap to match—what on earth was he doing, floundering about in the forest, late on an April afternoon? Titch, ploughing stolidly after him through the wettest and stickiest places, and covered with mud from top to toe, could have laughed aloud at his antics. People who were

scared of a bit of dirt, shouldn't choose this time of year
for a stroll. . . .

Crash!

What on earth was that? Even Titch started at the
sudden noise; the effect on the old gentleman was electric.
He plunged forward; nearly lost his footing, recovered
himself, and waving Titch on, began to trot down the
steeply descending track.

Smash! Crash!

The noise, twice repeated, came from not far ahead of
them. The lanky figure, jerking like a puppet between
the still trunks of the trees, all arms and legs and wild,
uncontrolled movements, blundered on even faster and
Titch, clutching his bicycle, followed close behind.
Someone must be breaking things in the middle of the
wood! And the old fellow in front was going so fast—so
fast he could surely never stop himself! Why were they
running like this? What was it all about, anyway? And
Titch, guffawing helplessly, began to choke with laughter
as he ran.

Their pace at last slackened as the slope eased off, and
through the barrier of trees the open meadow gleamed
fresh and green. Too much out of breath to speak, the
old gentleman motioned Titch to leave his bicycle and
follow him into the thicket. As quickly as they could,
they worked their way through the bushes.

Crash! Batter! Smash! The noise, redoubled and almost
continuous, sounded very close to them. The colours of a
caravan caught Titch's eye; they were coming out of the
trees, now, out into the open fields, and this, of course,
was the gypsies' camp. But what was happening? What
was all the noise about? And something was burning—
why, the waggon was alight! Side by side, half-hidden

behind the trunk of an oak, they stood on the fringe of
the forest and gazed across at the caravan and the crowd
of people gathered there. The old man was breathing
deeply and noisily, but his keen glance missed nothing
that was going on; and strange indeed were the happen-
ings on that stretch of level grassland. A sudden drift of
smoke swirled across and the acrid smell of burnt paint
reached their nostrils. The outline of the caravan was
ringed with fire; flames dancing from the roof and
walls.

Titch stared and stared again, and turning to ask an
urgent question, found that his companion had produced
a small blue notebook and pencil and was filling a blank
page with urgent jottings. The heading caught Titch's
eye, for the words were boldly underlined. He read them
twice before their meaning sank home. *Funeral Pyres*.

"D'you mean to say . . ." he began in an excited
undertone. He got no further with his question. A dog
had started to whine excitedly over by the crowd of
gypsies; standing, bristling at the forest edge, nose
pointing towards the trees. For some time it had made
short rushes into the thicket, and grew more and more
violent and noisy. Two or three of the men were wandering across to see what was the matter, and at that moment
the leader made a quick dive and disappeared into the
undergrowth. He emerged almost immediately, holding
by the arm a small boy, fair-haired and slightly built, who
shuffled unwillingly by the side of his captor.

Michael! Titch's eyes nearly popped out of his head.
So that was where he had got to! But what was going
to happen now? He should never have let himself be
caught like that, spying on the gypsies. And quite forgetting the old gentleman standing by his side, Titch

pushed quickly through the hazels, hopped the single strand of wire and set off at a run across the meadow.

Looking up and seeing him come, Michael felt greatly relieved. Now that Titch was on the warpath, things would very soon settle themselves. Those last few minutes, crouching practically inside a bush and hearing the dog whine frantically only a few yards away, had been little short of agony. He had tried to slip back into the forest and escape unnoticed, but his ankle had given him such a twinge that he had thought better of it, and stayed where he was. Now the three men were talking in their lingo with some of the others, and they were all staring at him in a very unfriendly way indeed. The biggest man still held his arm in a grip like a vice. What were they saying, he wondered. What were they going to do to him? Out of the corner of his eye he saw Titch coming round the black, charred shape of the waggon; the caravan still recognizable as such, but glowing and smoking; the heat shimmers twisting the trees behind and making them wriggle up into the sky like strands of waterweed caught in a current. There was no sign of Crusoe; there was no-one but gypsies here and no friendly face in all the group of Romany men and women.

"Leave my brother alone!" called Titch, galloping up, and he sounded really furious. "Let him go at once. You've no right . . ."

The group of gypsies turned towards him; dark eyes, dark bland faces giving away no hint of surprise or anger. Calmly they stared at him, and the women, bunched behind the men, poked their black, ostrich-feathered hats between their husband's shoulders and leisurely, appraisingly, took in the newcomer. Titch, very little daunted by their combined gaze, squared up before Michael's captor, and the gypsy, without releasing his grip, looked at him sardonically and did not speak. In size there was not much to choose between the two of them. Most of the other men were of slighter build, though they all looked wiry and as tough as leather. Titch realized that he stood no chance against them, but instinctively, he continued to bluff.

"Did you hear me?" He tried to speak as steadily as he could. "I said, let go of my brother. He's done nothing to you." He was breathing deeply; flushed with anger and excitement; his fists clenched.

The gypsy he was addressing turned and smiled at the man next to him; with a lift of his head and shrug of the shoulders that was quite plainly insolent. The smile passed from mouth to mouth and their scornful expressions goaded Titch beyond all endurance. Stung by their taunts, his blood up, he did a very foolish thing. Oblivious of the odds against him, he launched himself in blind fury against the gypsy and wrenched his hand from Michael's arm. Taken by surprise and unprepared for the assault, the man gave way, and stumbling over a foot behind him, tripped and fell.

Instead of the mass assault Titch feared, as a result of his action, a few of the younger men formed a circle and waited, pushing back those others who were pressing forward indignantly, voicing their protests. Scarcely had the gypsy touched the ground, his hat rolling off, than he bounded upright again with all the resilience of a rubber ball. His expression was not good to look upon, and Titch, braced to meet him, felt a momentary chill as he saw his opponent's face, almost black with anger; eyes burning, greasy hair tousled and falling over his brow.

They clinched; the gypsy springing and gripping like a

tiger, and Titch rocked on his heels with the force of the impact. He was strong for his age, and heavily built, but no boy of seventeen, however tough he may think himself, stands a chance against a man hardened by years of strenuous activity. He struggled desperately; calling on every ounce of energy he possessed, and held the gypsy for a few, long-drawn-out moments. Then his muscles gave slightly, he began to lose his balance, and with a cunning shift of hand and foot, his opponent took quick advantage and flung him down upon the meadow grass.

The gypsies shouted applause and narrowed their circle. Titch lay for a moment, dazed and shaken by this second fall in the space of ten or fifteen minutes. He was not prepared for the assault which followed almost at once, for he was accustomed to a code of fair play, and a man down was never set upon until he stood up again. The gypsy, however, had not been educated along the same lines, and from his point of view, an opponent on the ground was fair and legitimate prey! So he launched himself upon the powerless Titch and proceeded to use his fists and boots with great gusto, until Michael could bear it no longer and, forgetting his ankle, advanced hesitantly to the rescue. His efforts, slight though they were, gave Titch the chance he badly needed, and he was struggling up; Michael holding on as best he could, when a clear, impressive voice, issuing an order in words they could not understand, brought proceedings to a standstill. The circle of men and women broke up and separated the assailants; the gypsy was dusted down, his hat returned to him, and Michael, looking about him, bewildered, saw an oldish man, neatly dressed in a tweed suit; silver hair showing beneath his cap; a walking-stick in his hand; an old gentleman who had appeared from goodness knew where; not one of the Romany people, that was obvious, yet someone who spoke their language and whom they seemed ready to obey.

Titch, aching all over from blows and kicks received, recognized his late acquaintance and stared at him, as bewildered as Michael. The old gentleman repeated his words with conviction; shaking his stick towards the fire. The gypsies nodded; a few of them mumbled replies. They all seemed somewhat abashed. He was obviously telling them off, thought Titch; their faces wore the chastened expression of scolded children and only a very few showed any resentment. Then, with another sharp look, taking in the whole assembly, the stranger moved away from them towards the forest edge; upright and dignified as ever, walking as precisely as if his steps were leading him down the pavement of Pall Mall or Piccadilly.

Titch and Michael stared after him, open-mouthed. Behind them the gypsies were talking together in low voices. One or two of the men approached the boys again, but this time their intentions were friendly.

"He's not—he can't surely be a gypsy?" asked Titch, curiosity overcoming his resentment. "I was talking to him just now, in the forest."

"Indeed no, brother," came the answer. "Mr. Crawley is not one of us. But he is a clever man. You do not often find *his* like among the *gorgios*. Years we have known him and he has known our people. He is a true Romany *rai.*"

"He means to say, one who knows our speech and customs, brother," chimed in a little man standing close by. "There have been few such. As a rule, *gorgios* and Romany *chals* do not mix."

Michael turned at the sound of his voice and saw a

small, hunched figure; met the stare of pert, black eyes.
The gypsy's cap was pulled down half over his face, and
set at a jaunty, truculent angle, the peak almost resting
on the bridge of his beaky nose. As he looked at him,
Michael remembered the descriptions he had heard;
Crusoe, the twins, the D.'s telling of their Romany
friends. . . .

"I have known *gorgios* myself," the little man continued, and, suddenly certain, Michael interrupted his
next remark.

"I say!" he cried, very excited. "I'm sure you know
our friends. They've told us so much about you. You
bought Crusoe, Mr. Robinson, his waggon, didn't you?
Perhaps you can tell us where he is, now. You are his
friend, aren't you? You *are* Patch Cooper?"

CHAPTER 4

Claiming a Cousin

THE waggon walls had crumbled and fallen in. The wheels now carried only a blackened mound of ashes and charred remains, still pulsing a heart of red. Bent at a crazy angle, the stove pipe stuck up and out of the wreckage, and the grass all around was littered with grey-white fragments. The sky, dark and lowering close over the tree tops, let fall a few drops of rain, which spat and hissed in the glowing ruin of the caravan. The gypsies were still grouped together in a half-circle; standing in silence close to the comforting warmth. They seemed hypnotized; drugged with the heat; eyes reflecting the tiny pin points of brilliant crimson that came and went, flickered, leapt and disappeared deep in the powdered ash.

Titch and Michael, standing a little apart with Patch Cooper, had been listening to the gypsies' low-voiced explanations; watching the while the funeral pyre blaze up and die away as the evening thickened around them and the sky filled with ominous, blue-black clouds. Quietly, he had told them of this age-long custom of true gypsies; a custom which, fast dying out, was still occasionally practised. Urania Pinfold, whose waggon this had been, came of an old family, and before her death she had expressed a desire that all her possessions should be burnt or destroyed. That afternoon the gypsies had attended her funeral service; afterwards they had returned to carry out her wish. Her sisters, themselves, had smashed her utensils; waggon and harness were now burnt, later they would return, when the ashes were cold, and break the wheels and destroy, as best they could, the stove, the iron bondings, springs and other metal parts.

The brothers had listened with growing interest, mingled with amazement that such things should be. Now, with the dusk falling in earnest, Titch bestirred himself.

"We *must* get our bicycles," he said. "We won't b able to see anything in a minute, and we're still some miles from Dalehurst. How's your ankle feeling?" he asked, turning to Michael.

"Not too good," Michael had to admit, shifting his weight and testing his bad foot.

Here Patch Cooper interrupted them. "Don't you be thinkin' of it," he said, and his walnut face wrinkled knowingly. "I've a *lue* across in the camp, not a minute's walk from here, and you're very welcome to sleep by my fire. Fetch your bicycles, brother, and you'll be reaching Dalehurst to-morrow with the sun to warm your backs. We shall have heavy rain before the night's an hour older."

Titch looked at Michael and then they both turned to thank the little gypsy, but he would have none of it.

"A friend of Mr. Robinson's a friend o' mine," he said. "He was tellin' me, when I saw him last, that some of his *chavies* were to be visitin' soon. And, indeed, it seemed odd to find him alone in his waggon."

As Titch ran off to hunt for the bicycles, Michael asked Patch Cooper how he had found Crusoe. Whereabouts in Dalehurst was he camping?

"He's changed his pitch these two days," the gypsy replied. "I put him on to a better ground myself. You follow the Forest Road through the town and over on the far side, just beyond the houses, there's an inn, painted white it is, with a big sign hanging over the door. *The Royal Oak.* You can't miss it. And across the road there's a fine level space o' grass; a green with the trees all around, and that's where you'll find him."

Michael nodded; that should be an easy place for them to reach to-morrow. Then another thought struck him. He moved a little closer and spoke in a low voice.

"Won't the others mind us coming back with you, to the camp? They didn't much like . . ."

But Patch Cooper shook his head. "They don't mean no harm," he said gruffly. "Levi would have let you go soon enough, if your brother hadn't tried to boss him to it. He won't bear any ill will."

"What was it, the old gentleman said?" Michael persisted, still curious.

The gypsy looked at the ground; his mouth twisted wryly. Then he lifted his gaze. "He was right," he admitted frankly. " 'Twas neither time nor place to start fighting, with *gorgios* nor no-one, and he did well to cool our blood and remind us where we were."

Michael hunched himself deep into his coat collar. The rain was starting to fall more heavily and the clouds seemed to brush over his head; the line of trees was a smudge of inky blackness. Would Titch ever find the bicycles? He stared impatiently through the dusk and, in the silence, the moist wind seemed to bring to his ears the sound of a far-off, steady tapping. Somewhere a horse was trotting along a road; somewhere away beyond those trees where the shadows lay thick under the trunks. He listened idly, and then the wind breathed new sounds; the swish of wet branches and the patter and sigh of rain sweeping over the meadow grass, while a pony and trap, unbeknown to him, jogged comfortably on along the little lane that wound into the forest; with all three passengers dry and sheltered under the spread of a giant umbrella.

Your cousin Cynthia! Meeting the bus! Derek had enough to think about; sitting pressed between his sister and the vast bulk of the talkative old woman. She never ceased to chatter to them, and he listened carefully, trying to pick up useful tit-bits of information. But where were the brother and sister, Cynthia's proper cousins, who were coming to spend a week with her? Perhaps they were waiting somewhere in Littlecombe? Clearly, this person had never seen them before, for she in no wise suspected she carried the wrong passengers. But they would arrive at the house soon, and then, of course, the game would be up. There would be trouble at once, and they would be no better off and not much nearer the Royal Oak.

The raindrops were bouncing off the umbrella; falling heavily now; steadily and wetly falling on the sodden back of the cob who never faltered in his steady jog trot forward between the hedges. If they were to stop and explain themselves, down they would have to step into the road again and plod long miles through the pouring rain, as soaked and dripping as the unfortunate pony. And yet, by keeping up the pretence, they were only storing up more and more trouble for themselves. Derek's brow furrowed; he thought and thought again. Was there no third way out? This was an awkward situation, but if he puzzled his head for long enough he might have a brainwave. Little by little an idea began to form and take shape in his mind. The lady driving them, Mrs.

Potts she had called herself in the course of her conversation, seemed a kindly and helpful sort of person, and could be relied upon to be sympathetic. But he must play his cards carefully.

". . . and Mr. Crawley," Mrs. Potts continued without a pause for breath. "Mr. Crawley, he happens to come in from his afternoon constitutional—a great one for walks is your uncle and keeps hisself remarkable fit for an old gentleman, he was sixty-five last birthday though you wouldn't say so to look at him—and he says to me, Mrs. Potts he says, you're not going without the umbrella are you? he says, it'll be raining before you reach Littlecombe, mark my words. And sure enough, Master Philip, it rained cats and dogs before I reached the churchyard. I should have been soaked to the skin!"

"Master Philip" winced slightly. "It's about raining elephants now, isn't it?" he remarked, piling on the agony. A lash of rain on the drum-tight, black silk above them seemed to bear out his words.

Mrs. Potts quivered gently; she must have been laughing away down inside the shawls and rugs and overcoats.

"Indeed it is, that!" she rumbled. "Deary me, you always were a one! I remember when you were just three . . ."

Derek felt he couldn't bear another word. "It's a long time since you've seen us, isn't it?" he hazarded. Diana listened to him, aghast; wondering how he could dare to skate on ice as dangerously thin as this. But Mrs. Potts swung off at the desired tangent.

"A long time! You can well call it a long time!" she exclaimed. "You've grown a few inches in these nine years, I can tell you. Why, you were only so high, and Miss Margaret here was crawling about the floor. . . ."

"Would you have recognized us?" Derek growing very sure of himself, hastily put another spoke in her wheel, Diana bent forward instinctively and hid her face in her hands.

"I'd 've recognized you anywhere," asserted Mrs. Potts with regrettable confidence, adding in an undertone, "Not but what it isn't getting darkish now, but I've an eye for faces. Mr. Crawley, he often says to me . . ."

"How far are we from Mr.—from Uncle's house?" asked Derek.

"Matter of two miles," came the answer. "We reckon we're three from Littlecombe."

"Are you near the Forest Road; the main road to Dalehurst?" Derek was working gradually to the point.

"Why, that would be about a mile or so farther on," said Mrs. Potts, a little surprised at the question. A sudden gust of wind lifted the side of the umbrella and the rain drove viciously across them, stinging their hands.

"Awful to be walking in all this," Derek remarked gloomily. "We were lucky you gave us a lift when you did."

Mrs. Potts rumbled deep-throated agreement and pulled the umbrella straight again.

"Don't you feel sorry for everybody outside?"

Mrs. Potts seemed to think that all sensible people would stay in their homes on an evening like this.

"But suppose someone *had* to get somewhere. Suppose you were three or four miles from where you wanted to be and had to walk there? Wouldn't it be awful?"

Mrs. Potts agreed that it would. Diana saw where the conversation was leading, and held her breath. Sometimes Derek was almost *too* clever and made her feel really uncomfortable.

"Suppose," said Derek, playing the ace card of this particular suit. "Suppose you met two more children, like us, and they had to walk as far as that through the rain, all by themselves. Would you let them? What would you do?"

Mrs. Potts swallowed the bait whole. Her heart, large and warm, was stirred by the sorrowful picture Master Philip had drawn. What a dear, thoughtful boy he was, to be sure. And emphatically she took complete charge of the imaginary pair.

This was what Derek was waiting for. Their protection guaranteed, now was the time to reveal their true identity. And without hesitation, he grasped the nettle, while Diana sat by him, tongue-tied and unhappy.

"Well, we do want you to help us," he said. "You see, we *are* strangers. We're not called Philip and Margaret and Mr. Crawley isn't our uncle. We haven't ever heard of him or Cynthia before. We want to get to the big tree in the forest, the Royal Oak, where a friend of ours is camping with his caravan. And we missed the bus and hitch-hiked instead, and the lorry took us the wrong way. Please will you drive us to the Forest Road? We shall be able to find our way from there and it won't be so far."

The pony, pulled up sharply, slithered about on the wet road, and the trap stopped with a jerk. The large bundle turned and a red, round face, eyes framed in wire spectacles, gazed indignantly down at them. Bewilderment turned to anger; anger gradually gave way to pained surprise. Then, deep in her throat, Mrs. Potts began to chuckle.

"You're having me on, Master Philip. You're pulling old Potty's leg! Miss Cynthia, she do torment me some-

thing awful, and I'll not know if I'm standing on my head or my heels!"

"No, I'm not. Really and truly not. I'm Derek Longmore, and this my sister Diana. I don't know where the others are, we didn't see them at Littlecombe. We came in a lorry, and when it stopped outside an inn, we got down and walked along this road. He wasn't taking us the right way."

"You were in that lorry? I wouldn't have thought it possible! And for goodness sakes where's Master Philip and Miss Margaret? Mr. Crawley will have something to say to me for this! Oh deary, deary me!"

"Perhaps they haven't come after all," Diana suggested, feeling desperately sorry for the unfortunate Mrs. Potts. "I'm sure you'd have seen them in the village if they had been on the bus."

"They were coming Friday," was all Mrs. Potts could repeat in a doleful voice, shaking her head slowly from side to side. "They wrote they were a'coming Friday."

"But to-day's Thursday," said Derek, on the spot as usual. "I know, because the *Sorcerer* comes out to-day. I bought this week's copy at the station this morning." And he dug from one of his pockets a crumpled "blood" with a lurid cover. "Look," he said, producing a torch and directing the beam on to the front page, "there's the date."

Mrs. Potts adjusted her spectacles and gazed with interest at the picture thus revealed, shown up in all it's plentiful detail. A man was hanging, head downwards, from a low-flying aircraft, linking hands with a youth perched hazardously upon the boiler of a railway engine hurtling along the metals just beneath. A few yards ahead the line plunged, without warning, into an abyss.

"Terrible," said Mrs. Potts, pursing her lips. "Looks dangerous to me. I don't hold with these new-fangled ways of travel. Pony and trap used to be good enough for most people. Mr. Crawley, he doesn't believe in motor cars."

"But the date," Derek reminded her. "It says Thursday, doesn't it?"

Mrs. Potts had to agree that it did.

"Well!" she exclaimed. "I don't know what could have come over me. To think I should go wrong like that! So it's to-morrow they should be here. Well, well, well!" And she began to shake slightly, laughing at her own stupidity.

"That makes it all right for us, then," pounced Derek. "I mean, you'll take us to the Forest Road?"

"To be sure I can," was the reply, and with a flap of the reins they were off again; joggling between the hedges to the steady beat of hooves.

Derek sat back, contented, but old Mrs. Potts would not let him be. She wanted to know all about them, and who was this friend of theirs and why he was camping in the forest. Derek explained as best he could, and told her again where Crusoe was to be found. She knew the tree he meant, she said, but it was a tidy way from the road and the track would be ankle deep in mud after all this rain. She tut-tutted a good deal; said that it was getting proper dark and not a fit time for children to be wandering in the forest, and so they drove on along the lonely road, meeting no-one, the rain continually pattering down; every now and then a heavy drip from one of the trees plopping on to the umbrella. At last the pony's even pace slowed, and without waiting for Mrs. Potts to move the reins he turned off sharp to the right, through the small stone pillars of a gateway. The wheels crunched the rough surface of a drive.

"Here!" cried Derek. "This isn't the way. You said you were going to take us . . ."

He stopped abruptly, for the dark masses of laurels and evergreens parted and revealed a row of gleaming windows; oblongs of bright yellow throwing a faint light over the lawn and the drive. On they trotted, coming round to the steps leading up to the front door.

Derek wanted to leap down from the trap as it moved, and vanish into the shrubbery, but with Diana to look after, and their rucksacks, escape was not so easy. This was treachery, of course—Mrs. Potts meant to give them up to Mr. Crawley and then anything might happen. At all costs they must get away. But a cheerful rumble from the large figure next to him broke in upon his thoughts.

"This'll be better for you mites than gallivanting about the forest this hour of the evening. A good, hot supper and a warm bed for you both, and you shall be put on your way to-morrow. You leave it to me and don't worry yourselves. Miss Cynthia, she'll enjoy this bit of fun, and Mr. Crawley, he won't know any different till he meets his proper pair of nephews and nieces!" Mrs. Potts' huge frame shook, and still chuckling she drew up before the stone porch of the house.

That's all very well, thought Derek, but we can't hang about here and stop the night in a strange house. This woman was becoming a positive nuisance. If she wouldn't drive them to the Forest Road, they must walk it, that's all. Then he remembered his sister and felt a pang of conscience. It was still pouring with rain, and as Mrs. Potts began to heave herself out of the trap, the umbrella tilted again and a jet of water slid over him. He brushed his hand impatiently across his hair and several drops trickled down his neck. Perhaps, after all . . . He heard Diana gratefully accepting the kind offer that had been made them and he opened his mouth to protest. The wind and rain stung his cheek and ear. He said nothing, but climbed meekly to the ground and, rucksack over his shoulder, followed his sister up the glistening steps.

After a change into dry stockings and bedroom slippers, Derek felt better. After a really nice supper—for Mrs. Potts had spared herself no trouble and had prepared a lavish welcome for the long-absent Philip and Margaret— he felt better still. They ate by themselves, in a small room; their table drawn close to a roaring log fire, and the old lady, now emerged from her chrysalis of shawls and overcoats, popped in and out with one succulent dish after another, and made apt comments upon each as she placed it before them.

"First potatoes from the garden," she announced, taking off a lid and revealing in a cloud of steam the pile of the small golden vegetables, some of them no bigger than marbles. A roast leg of lamb was carved; then a large covered dish was placed revently upon the table, and "Asparagus" whispered Mrs. Potts. "Help yourselves, now, and don't leave any." And later, after a magnificent trifle and cream, Derek lay back in his chair and stretched his legs in sleepy trance. Crusoe and caravaning seemed far, far away indeed.

"I wonder where the others are," Diana said, half to herself, at the end of the meal. Certainly, it seemed curious that no-one should have yet greeted them. She asked Mrs. Potts, when that lady came in to see if they had had enough of everything, and received a nod and a mysterious smile for answer.

"Mr. Crawley, he works in his study of an evening," she explained, later, clearing away the plates. "He's partikler busy to-night and when you goes to see him, you'll please not to stay long."

Derek and Diana hastily assured her that their stay with their uncle would be of the shortest possible duration.

"After that you can come upstairs and meet Miss Cynthia," Mrs. Potts continued.

"Upstairs?" said Diana. "Is she ill, then?"

"No Miss, she goes to bed early as a rule. Miss Cynthia . . ." And here the old lady's face fell. "She isn't what you'd call strong. Not a strong child, she isn't, like you are."

Derek and Diana, suddenly conscious of glowing cheeks and tremendous appetites, only lately assuaged, felt almost ashamed to be as robust as they were. And yet, when compared with their friends the Sanville twins, Brian and Pamela, they were always considered "pale and interesting." Anyway, Titch had said so once, in one of his teasing moods!

"Oh dear, I *am* sorry," said Diana, and Derek echoed his sister.

"Now you come along o' me and I'll show you Mr. Crawley's study." Mrs. Potts became bustling and motherly again. "Don't you worry, and don't you talk much. When Mr. Crawley's busy he doesn't notice things, and he hasn't seen Master Philip and Miss Margaret these last nine years, no more than I have."

Feeling very little reassured, Derek and Diana followed Mrs. Potts along a passage. They were both trembling about the knees when she stopped by a door and gave the panel a sharp rap. She had to knock again before she received an answer. Then she popped her head inside, introduced them in a flustered manner, and turning abruptly, almost shoo'd them into the room. She really might have been driving geese, thought Derek, stumbling after his sister.

Standing on the border of a long carpet, they gazed down between the walls lined with bookshelves to the lamplit desk at the far end. The bulb had a green shade and this made everything else dim and shadowy, but threw a pool of bright light on to the pages Mr. Crawley was studying. His pen was raised; his head lowered; his hair glinted silver in the edge of the radiance. They waited, and still he did not look up. Then he began to write, and the room was so quiet that they heard distinctly the scratch of his pen as the nib moved over the paper. They both felt embarrassed, not knowing quite what to do. Derek gave a slight cough and shuffled his feet.

The pen stopped and Mr. Crawley peered round the lamp; dazzled by the brightness.

"Come closer," he said. "Let me see you."

When they approached to within a yard of the desk, he moved the shade so that the light fell upon them. "Yes," he murmured. "You've changed a great deal." His eyes searched their faces and Diana blinked nervously and swallowed. "Do people say you resemble your mother or your father?" he inquired of Derek.

"Neither," Derek managed to gulp.

"For once I'm inclined to agree with the majority! But now I must ask you to leave me, for as you see I have a great deal of work to do. I had an interesting experience this afternoon." For a moment he seemed about to describe his experience to them, but he recovered

C

himself and turned down the shade of the lamp so that
only the top of his desk was illuminated. "Good night,"
he said. "I shall see more of you to-morrow. I hope you
will enjoy your stay with us. Cynthia, I know, is looking
forward to meeting you again." And his pen began to
scratch once more, continuing the letter he was engaged
upon. "*To the President, Gypsy Lore Society,*" he had written.
"*This afternoon, in the Dalehurst area of the Forest, I witnessed
the funeral pyre of Urania Pinfold . . .*"

Dismissed, Derek and Diana shuffled across the carpet
and out of the room. Mrs. Potts was waiting for them
just along the passage.

"There's good children!" she breathed. "You didn't
stay any time. Now if you'll come upstairs with me, I'll
show you your rooms and you can meet Miss Cynthia."

Brother and sister followed after her and found that
their bedrooms were next to each other. Each had a
brass knocker upon the door, shaped like a bird. Derek's
was an owl; Diana's a peacock, tail outspread.

"There's beauty and wisdom for you," Mrs. Potts
remarked with a chuckle, making them both blush.

They dumped their rucksacks and then followed her
across to the other side of the house. A door, slightly ajar,
showed a chink of light. This, evidently, was Cynthia's
room.

"I'll go first," whispered Mrs. Potts, creeping impressively forward. "Just in case the little lamb's asleep."

Derek and Diana, catching the sick-room atmosphere,
tip-toed close behind her. With infinite care, the old
lady took hold of the handle and pushed open the door.

Clatter-wallop-bang! Without warning, an avalanche
descended on their shoulders. Books burst open everywhere, scattering their leaves. Mrs. Potts, in self-protec-

tion, flung her arms about her head, and Derek caught
a glimpse of a bright, keen little face, framed in a cluster
of red curls, peering out from the bed in the far corner;
gleefully anticipating this moment of triumph. But at that
instant her expression changed.

"Oh, Potty!" she cried. "I *am* so sorry! I meant it for
the others, not for you. Why did you have to get in
the way?"

CHAPTER 5

Findings' Keepings

WHILE Derek and Diana made themselves useful, picking up the bits and pieces of the booby trap from the floor, Mrs. Potts, lowering her arms from her head and by now fully recovered from her first shock, began to scold Cynthia with all the resources at her command. How could she have done such a thing; with her poor dear mother away and trusting her to be a good girl. She was not in the slightest worried about any damage that might have been inflicted on herself or even upon Cousins Philip and Margaret. What really seemed to astound her was that Cynthia, unaided, had succeeded in perching the pile of books on the top of the door. Derek privately thought this a little unfair. He had been hit on the head by a large, hard book. He picked it up and looked at the lettering on the leather binding. *Smith's Latin Dictionary*. He thought as much.

After Cynthia had promised faithfully never, under any circumstances, to attempt such a thing again, Mrs. Potts retired; still ruffling her feathers like an angry hen. Derek and Diana were left alone with their "cousin," and stood, a little awkwardly, by her bedside. For a long moment no-one said anything. Cynthia stared straight ahead, without seeing them, her face gradually darkening. Then, with a twist, she buried herself in her pillow and burst into tears.

This was a bad beginning, and Derek left his sister to deal with the emergency. Diana succeeded so far, that in a minute or two Cynthia raised her head and, with streaming eyes, chokingly tried to explain what was the matter.

"I'm never allowed to do anything I want," she said between gulps. "Nothing I like is ever 'good' for me and I'm tired of being different. I want to be the same as everyone else and do the things they do."

Diana tried to cheer her up, but Cynthia refused to be consoled and sniffed miserably to herself and blew her nose. Then, as suddenly as it had come, the storm passed and she smiled again.

"It *was* funny, seeing you all jump," she said. "Poor old Potty! Just like her to get in the way. Did anything hit you?"

Derek felt it was time at least one of the victims obtained a little sympathy.

"Feel here," he said, bending over her and indicating the spot on his head with outstretched finger. "I've got a bump coming up already. It'll be bigger still before long."

Cynthia felt the bump and burst out laughing when he told her what had caused it. "I *hate* Latin," she said. "I'm so glad it's given you a headache, too!"

Derek retired, nursing his injured dignity.

"I say!" Cynthia cried, turning to Diana. "Potty said you'd got a secret to tell me. She wouldn't say what it was about. I can keep secrets, Margaret, honestly I can!"

Diana hesitated. "You promise not to tell," she began at last. "Not to tell anyone on your word of honour. It's very important."

Cynthia promised; very solemn; her eyes wide.

"Well, we aren't your cousins," Diana announced, and Derek stood at the foot of the bed and said stiffly, "My name's Derek Longmore. My sister's called Diana."

Cynthia looked from one to the other; half inclined to be frightened, half to laugh.

"Then why are you here?" she asked. "Why did Potty let you come in? Where *are* Philip and Margaret? You're not telling whoppers, are you?" And a mischievous gleam lit her eyes.

Derek, still on his dignity, assured her they were not. Diana began to explain, and Cynthia listened, lips parted, hair all tangled up, eyes still red from crying. She must be about the same age as they were, Diana thought to herself even as she told their story; and although her face was small and a bit pinched, her expression was keen as a needle and she never missed a word. If she hadn't looked so frail, she might have been very pretty indeed.

"And Mrs. Potts made us come in and spend the night here," Diana concluded. "And to-morrow we'll go and find Crusoe—Mr. Robinson—at the Royal Oak. Perhaps we'll meet Patch Cooper again. He's a gypsy and a great friend of ours," she added impressively. But, for once, Cynthia did not bat an eyelid.

"My Daddy knows lots of gypsies," she said. "So do I. He's often taken me with him, when he goes down to the camp. There was a big fire this afternoon, and they burnt a caravan."

"Yes, that's right," nodded Diana, not believing a word, but Cynthia was a great deal too sharp to be taken in.

"There *was*," she insisted. "I know you don't believe me, and it's beastly of you. I believed all you said, about the lorry and everything. I'll take you to the camp to-morrow, if you'll push my chair, and then you can just see!"

She was so earnest that even Derek was impressed. "Camp?" he said. "Where? Perhaps Crusoe . . ."

"Daddy will know." The little girl was irritatingly calm and certain. "He knows all about the gypsies."

"How far away are they?" Derek was prepared to leave that very instant.

"Down in the valley below our garden," Cynthia told him, and then sensing his purpose, cried, "You mustn't go now. I want you to take me to-morrow. You can't . . ."

Derek looked at his sister. "Might be worth trying," he said, ignoring the protests from the bed.

"It's still raining," said Diana doubtfully. "And black as pitch. He might not be there, after all. Let's go to-morrow."

"Oh, please do, *please!*" begged Cynthia. "Don't go away now. I want you to take me. Daddy hasn't taken me for weeks and Potty never goes anywhere except on the roads." This last was voiced with withering scorn.

Reluctantly, Derek allowed himself to be persuaded. They then talked gypsies solidly and discovered how much Cynthia really knew. Her knowledge and experience, for all her handicaps, went far deeper than theirs. The D.'s found that, so far, they had only scratched the surface. Evidently, Mr. Crawley had written several books about the Romany tribes in England, and his daughter had learnt a great deal from him. Then the bustling figure of Mrs. Potts appeared; smiling and cheerful again, to be greeted with a howl of wrath from Cynthia.

"Oh, go *away*, Potty! We don't want you here!"

But all her expostulations were of no avail and did not in the slightest disturb the old lady's smiling expression.

Derek and Diana were packed off to their rooms and
Cynthia, still grumbling, was tucked up and settled for
the night.

"To-morrow!" she called after them, peering round
the all-eclipsing bulk, for Mrs. Potts was shaking up her
pillows. "To-morrow morning as soon as I get up. Don't
go away! Promise you won't start before I'm ready?"

They promised, and saying good night, found their
way along the passage, back to their own doors. Derek
idly fingered the cold brass owl.

"Funny thing, she should know so much about gypsies,"
he murmured. "I wonder what's wrong with her. She
doesn't *look* ill."

Diana disagreed with him. "You can see there's something the matter," she said. "I do like her. I think she's
such fun."

Mrs. Potts, following them along the passage at that
moment, their remarks were interrupted.

"You'll be ready for bed, I expect," she remarked.
"Miss Cynthia, she was proper tired, though she wouldn't
admit it. She's a rare pluck'd 'un, she is. It's a treat for
her to have some mites of her own age to play with,
instead of us old fogies."

Derek controlled his indignation as best he could.
"Play," indeed!

"How she got them books up on that door, I couldn't
say," Mrs. Potts continued. "But she's a wicked girl to
do such a thing. She might have killed herself."

The D.'s looked at each other, a little incredulous. The
doors, after all, were not as high as that. If you stood on a
chair, the tops were within easy reach.

"You wouldn't understand, of course. 'Tisn't natural
for strong, healthy children. The poor mite is paralysed,

you see." Mrs. Potts lowered her voice almost to a whisper. "She can't stand up, not without holding on to something. No power in her legs, no power at all. And," shaking her head sadly, "she'll never be no better."

Derek and Diana went to bed in a sober frame of mind. They both lay awake for some while, thinking about Cynthia and how difficult her life must be. Hitherto they had never thought much about their bodies. Legs and arms were made to be used, and they had always used them. But not to be able to stand up; not to walk; at their age! To imagine oneself in such a situation was almost unbearable. And next morning the realities of being a cripple were brought home to them very vividly indeed.

They had finished their breakfast, sitting together in the same little room where they had eaten the night before. So far they had seen nothing of Cynthia or Mr. Crawley. Outside the window spread a garden; lawns and flower-beds leading down a gentle slope to a border of tall trees, grey-brown and shining in the sunlight. The clouds had cleared in the night; all trace of the storm had blown away and the world was fresh and gleaming, wet and brilliant under an arch of light blue sky. The day invited them to start on their travels!

Suddenly they heard a shuffling and a bumping noise outside. Derek opened the door and, Diana following, rushed across the hall and up the first flight, two at a time, for there at the top lay Cynthia, sprawled head foremost down the stairs.

But "Go away!" she cried. "Leave me alone. I'm quite all right. This is my way. I invented it myself." And without more ado she proceeded down the stairs; putting a hand on each step and dragging her legs after her.

c*

Derek and Diana retreated, and when she reached the hall bent to pick her up. Again she snapped at them, and helplessly they stood on each side of her as she crawled slowly over the carpet and through the open door. Once inside, she began, inch by inch, to pull herself up into a chair. Derek was about to lend a hand; it was tantalizing just to stand and watch her laborious efforts, but Diana caught hold of him in the nick of time.

"Don't," she exclaimed in a whisper. "Let's sit down and try not to notice."

And that was probably the hardest thing they had done in all their lives.

Almost as Cynthia had settled herself comfortably, Mrs. Potts burst into the room, very out of breath and red in the face.

"How did you get here?" she puffed. "Oh, Miss Cynthia, you didn't come crawling down them stairs again, did you? Why, Potty was going to fasten your irons for you, and then you could have come down like a lady."

Cynthia only sniffed. To be a lady evidently appealed very little, or perhaps Mrs. Potts had used the phrase so often that it had worn a little thin.

"I didn't want to wait," she said. "And now I'd like to be put in my chair. Philip—Derek I mean, and Diana, wasn't it?—are going to take me to the gypsies' camp."

"Indeed they are! Will you let Potty fix your irons for you, first, and . . ."

"No!" cried Cynthia. "You know I hate those beastly things. I want to go just as I am."

Mrs. Potts bent down and lifted her in her arms, with much gasping and belaboured breathing. "Getting too heavy, you are, though I've carried you since you was a baby. Up with you, then!" And she staggered with her into the hall. By the front door stood a small wheeled chair, rather like an outsize collapsible pram, and here Mrs. Potts settled her, sending Derek for a cushion to put behind her back.

Mrs. Potts insisted on helping them down the steps. Once safely on the drive, she let Derek take charge, warning him to go carefully and be a good boy; which advice Derek accepted with as much good grace as he could muster. Then, feeling absurdly self-conscious in this new rôle of nursemaid, he set off, pushing the chair; Diana walking alongside.

Cynthia knew the quickest and best way. Down the drive they went, up the road a short distance, and then turned into a lane, on the same side of the road as the house. After the downpour, the track was muddy, and strips of water lay in the ruts, reflecting the blue of the sky. Hazels and silver birches sloped from the thickets, and catkins, gold in the sunshine, hung from the slender twigs above their heads. On the green, mossy banks of the ditches grew occasional clumps of primroses, and the floor of the wood was starred with misty, white anemones. Diana picked flowers as they slowly made their way along the track, and soon Cynthia's lap was heaped with pale-coloured, delicate spring blossoms. She found a few purple orchis, their tapering leaves blotched with black, and added these to the collection; and violets, too, were to be discovered if you looked close enough, growing tight into the banks and hiding their flowers among blades of grass and under leaves.

Cynthia, her red hair still tangled and untidy for all Mrs. Pott's brushing, grew more and more lively; talking

away, missing nothing, and stretching out eager hands
for everything Diana picked. She made Derek stop the
chair and try and jump for a branch of catkins high
above his lifted arm, and shrieked with laughter when he
landed both feet in a puddle and spattered them all with
flying mud. She demanded wands of pussy willow, deep
inside the tangled undergrowth, and brother and sister
struggled with dead brambles and slithered on treacherous,
slimy patches; returning to her at last with the furry,
silver-shining buds. They were soon tired out, for Cynthia's demands were inexhaustible, and the chair was
hard to push through the soft mud. Never for a moment
did her interest flag. She was keyed up and as vibrant
as a bird, yet tight-gripped, like a bird held in the hand,
in the clutches of the wheeled chair. Pulsing with life,
she was shackled; a prisoner chained within the very
sight and feel of freedom.

Soon the path began to slope into the valley, and
through the trees they caught a glimpse of a long, narrow
stretch of green meadowland.

"The gypsies camp down there," Cynthia told them,
and as Derek held back the chair and gloomily anticipated
the return uphill, she began to sing in a clear, high voice.
She could go right through her songs, remembering all
the words and everything, thought Diana, which was
more than they could, except *John Peel* and easy ones
like that. She recalled their efforts at singing, last summer,
in the hills, sheltering from the rain in the little stone hut,
and laughed quietly to herself. Cynthia, still singing,
began to sort and bunch the flowers that covered her lap.
She seemed happy enough; yet she was surely too excited,
too worked up for it to last. People who were really
solidly happy were altogether calmer and quieter about

it. Or was it, wondered Diana, that she and her brother just happened to be quieter, solider people?

Cynthia was singing, now, something they could not understand. The tune was beautiful, but the words were not even in French, which Diana could have recognized easily enough, even if she had not been able to translate them.

"What was that?" she asked, when the song came to an end. "Can you talk in that language?"

Cynthia shook her head. "I can sing in Italian and I know what the words mean, because Mummy taught me," she said. "That's a boy's song, really, from *Figaro*—an opera by Mozart," she added, seeing that the name conveyed nothing to Diana. "Only nowadays a girl always sings it, dressed up as a boy."

"What's it all about?" Diana wanted to know.

"He's in love for the first time," Cynthia tried to explain, "and can't understand; he doesn't know what's happening, only that everything's different and changed and more beautiful. He just feels that he's bursting with something and *must* sing! Do listen, you can hear the song bubbling up inside him. I feel like that, this morning. It's so lovely here, I love the forest. . . ."

Derek, piloting the chair downhill, was busy with his own thoughts, and scarcely noticed that Cynthia had started to sing again. But Diana listened and understood what she meant; felt the song leap up, expressing the wonder and happiness of life. True enough, all the freshness and colour of the spring morning; the powerful, flowing gladness of being alive, were a part of this breathless music. She suddenly felt, through Cynthia, a small part of what it must be like to be a singer; to be someone who instinctively expresses themselves, their joys and sorrows and experiences, through song, instead of through the paintbrush of the artist or the pen of the poet and writer.

"Thank you," she said, when Cynthia had finished. "I wish I could sing as well as you can. Such a lot of people I know seem to be able to *do* things and I can only feel. Feel how nice everything is," she tried to make herself clear, "and not to be able to say so."

They came round a bend in the lane at that moment and found a gate ahead of them.

"We're nearly there," cried Cynthia. "Through the gate and then we shall see the caravans. Listen, we may be able to hear the noise they make."

They all stood in silence, but only the song of birds and the distant murmuring of a stream came gently to their ears. Echoing far away, they heard the double note twice, three times repeated, of a cuckoo.

They pushed on, Diana running ahead to undo the latch of the gate and swing it back, creaking on rusty hinges. They passed through, out on to the meadow, and Cynthia looked quickly to the left, bending forward as far as she was able.

"They've gone!" she cried. "We're too late. They've gone for the summer! Oh, *what* a shame."

They walked across in the direction she pointed out, and found the grass scarred and rutted with the tracks of wheels. Here was a loose turf, clumsily replaced over a hole dug for a cooking fire; there the grass was yellow and flattened in a pattern of squares and oblongs. The D.'s wandered disconsolately about, kicking at odd pieces of rubbish and discarded belongings; trying to picture the gypsy camp as it had been, the day before. Then Derek gave a sudden exclamation and bent to pick up something from the ground. Diana, going across to him, saw that he held a penknife in the palm of his hand.

"That's lucky," she said. "I suppose findings' keepings."

But Derek paid no attention to her remarks. He was staring at the knife, frowning. Then his face cleared and he looked up, choking with excitement.

"Of course!" he exclaimed. "I *knew* I'd seen it before. Look!" And he pointed to the little silver shield on the black side of the knife. The initials E.C. were intertwined there, engraved on the metal.

"E.C.," said Diana, puzzled. "We don't know anybody with . . ."

"We do!" cried Derek. "This is Titch's knife! Yes, Titch! Don't you know he's called Edward, really? He won this at school, for something or other, I forget what. Why he must have been camping here last night, about a mile away from us! Oh, if only, if *only* we'd known!"

CHAPTER 6

Invitation to the Dance

"THERE you are, brother! You could spend as snug a winter's night in a *lue* as in any of your stone-built houses." Patch Cooper bent over the ashes of his fire, and taking a few dry sticks, blew them into a flame. He added more wood and as the flames licked up, Titch and Michael gazed around the interior of the tent.

They had crawled in through a small opening in the canvas, following the little gypsy, and standing lost in pitch darkness, had dared scarcely to raise their heads, thinking the roof must be close above them. Now, in the dancing yellow light, they saw that the centre dome of the tent towered up, as high as a ceiling. A framework of tapering ash poles surrounded them, supporting the smoke-blackened canvas; thick ends driven into the earth; thin ends drawn together into the summit of the dome; and there must be a hole of some sort, for the smoke from the fire, placed centrally on the floor, rose in a steady column and disappeared. All around, the air was fresh. Patch Cooper had sealed the entrance behind them, and the shape of the tent acted as a chimney drawing up the fire.

As soon as the logs were burning steadily, the gypsy swung a black pot over the flames and then dragged forward stools for the boys to sit themselves down upon. Above the crackle of the fire they could hear the rain steadily falling on the sloping canvas walls.

"Come and dry yourselves," he said. "Put your bags on the floor there, and make yourselves comfortable.

The *hobben* will be ready soon." He removed the lid from the pot and stirred vigorously with a large spoon. " 'Tis a rare chance that you should have happened across Patch Cooper, and this the last night of our stay!"

"Are you moving so soon, then?" Michael asked him.

"Aye, brother, we've a long journey to make and we shall be started betimes. We've spent the winter in the forest, and now we must take to the road again." He stretched himself, lifted his arms above his head. "I reckon we're most itchin' to be off!" he added with a chuckle.

"Will you put up this big tent in a new place every night?" said Titch, still gazing around.

Patch Cooper shook his head. "We don't use a *lue*, not in the summer," he said. "Waggons or traps and rod tents——" He jerked a thumb over his shoulder. "We travels light and any who wants can sleep under the stars."

Michael and Titch, peering into the shadowy circumference, saw that another, smaller tent was attached to the *lue*. Vaguely, behind a half-drawn curtain, they made out the shape of a bed. So that was where the gypsy slept? He certainly had room enough; these were spacious quarters, indeed! No wonder they preferred a *lue* to live in through the winter months. This was definitely one up on Derek, Diana and the twins, thought Michael. They had never seen the inside of a tent like this; a tent with an open fire in the middle of the floor, and a hole in the roof to let out the smoke! He had never even realized such things existed! Looking at the swarthy-faced little man, squatting across on the far side of the flames; the dark, curving dome of the canvas rising around him; the column of smoke, tinged golden at the foot, then dove grey, then merging with the shadowy dusk beyond the light from the fire; he really had to remind himself that he was in England, and not in some other, stranger, part of the world.

"Mr. Cooper," said Titch, a little hesitantly. "The others told us about the camp fire, last summer, when they met you and a big man, I've forgotten what he was called."

"Reuben Hearne, brother," interrupted the gypsy. "Aye, he was there, I remember well."

"That's right," said Titch. "And you and Mr. Hearne played mouth-organs, didn't you? They said you played marvellously. Have you got yours with you? We should so like . . ."

Patch Cooper's face crinkled; he stared across the fire at them, and with his black eyes, hook nose and tousled hair, he looked more like a gnome than a man; some dweller in a cavern underneath the earth. Then he hunted around amongst his belongings and returned to crouch upon his stool again, holding the instrument to his mouth; hands completely covering it and hiding most of his face, too. Very softly and slowly, he began to spell out the lively rhythm of a dance, gradually increasing speed and volume, until the boys' very feet began to tap and their fingers to beat time instinctively. They heard voices outside the tent; someone, unsteadily, was singing the tune, and then a heavy body lurched against the canvas wall. Hands plucked away the sackcloth covering the entrance hole and the fire smoke swirled all ways as, following close on each others heels, three young gypsies pushed into the *lue*.

Tiddle-*ump*-iti-*ump*-iti-*ump!* Patch Cooper wagged his head and blew into the little instrument with all his

might. The newcomers footed it gravely round the fire,
behind the crouching figures of the gypsy and the two
gorgio brothers, and then, more and more hilariously,
tripping and lurching together, faster and faster, round
and round they stumbled and kicked; twisted and turned;
now holding on to each other, all three linked as one;
now spinning singly, dizzily revolving until the whole
tent seemed to turn on itself like a shadowy top!

Titch and Michael both gasped, as if for breath, when
with a final chord and flourish, Patch Cooper put an
end to the insistent rhythm and the dancers gyrated to
a standstill.

"Another tune, brother! Another tune!" one of the
men demanded, and plunging his hand into his trouser
pocket, he drew out a handful of loose coins. He flung
three or four pennies on the ground and, shuffling them
into position with his foot, challenged the others to
match his skill. As Patch Cooper started to play again,
he commenced a wonderfully light, agile dance, spinning
on his toes; kicking his legs high in the air; executing his
intricate movements always on the same spot.

"He's dancing on the pennies!" Michael whispered to
Titch. "He *is!* And scarcely moving them at all."

They glued their eyes to the gypsy's feet, for in the
shifting light from the fire it was hard to see what was
happening. At last the dancer waved his arm, the music
stopped, and with a final bound sideways he exposed the
coins, lying on the floor of the tent exactly where he had
placed them.

"Clever dodge, that," Titch grudgingly admitted. "If
he really was stepping on them."

But there seemed little doubt about it. One of the
other gypsies accepted the challenge and the indefatigable

Patch Cooper struck up a new tune. Almost at the first kick, however, one of the pennies went skidding across the ground, and though he danced with grim determination, the challenger could not tread lightly enough and gradually shuffled and dispersed the neat circle of coins. Finally, he hopped aside with an exclamation of disgust, and stood mopping his brow with a crimson handkerchief.

"Tell me," said the champion, stepping into the firelight. "Will your young friend here dance a round with me?" And he leered forward, bending over the Crosbies.

Titch looked up into the face close above him and recognized the features of his late adversary. The light had been dim; the dancers standing, for the most part, with their faces in shadow, and he had not noticed that this was the same man. Michael, too, looked up and felt suddenly cold, for all the heat from the flames. What had Patch Cooper said? "Levi won't bear any ill will," that was it. Michael only hoped he was right. Patch was on their side, of course, but was very small; really very little bigger than he was. And the dancing; was it just a blind then? Was this a trap and the three gypsies out for mischief? Titch, staring up, was thinking on very much the same lines as his brother. Had they run into trouble again? They were fools, probably, to have stayed here at all; and not plugged on and reached Dalehurst and Crusoe. Michael's ankle, of course . . . and still ruminating he began, very slowly, to get to his feet. There was silence in the *lue*; Patch Cooper had not yet answered, although the champion's question was addressed to him, rather than to Titch direct.

"I can't dance," said Titch, taking the bull by the horns, for he felt that something was expected of him.

"But I *can* do this." And measuring with a rapid glance
the height of the tent and the ground by the side of the
fire, he did a handstand, legs and feet together, body as
straight as he could make it. Then, curving his legs over
to the right, and adjusting his balance, he gradually
supported his weight on his right arm. Michael watched
him, holding his breath. This was one of his brother's
best tricks, but it required all his strength and steadiness,
and Titch, he knew, was stiff after the fight and the fall
from his bicycle. He was doing it, though! He was
doing it!

And Titch, for a few seconds, raised his left arm from
the ground and balanced himself, body and legs arched,
on the palm of his right hand. Then, once again supported
on both arms, he hand-walked right round the fire. As
he let his legs fall and crouched, resting after his efforts,
the gypsies murmured excitedly and the champion dancer
took off his coat and handed it to one of his friends.
Without a moment's hesitation he stood on his hands,
but his legs fell back and he had to kick up several times
before he was properly balanced and was able to hold
his position. Then, waveringly, he tried to shift his
weight, as Titch had done.

Both brothers shouted a warning together, for the
gypsy was dangerously near the fire; and unlike Titch,
who had swung himself away from the flames, he was
drooping his legs right over the burning logs. He was only
just keeping his balance and had not yet removed one of
his hands. He gave a lurch and seemed on the point of
falling. Titch sprang forward, collided violently with
another would-be rescuer, and with a yell the gypsy
crashed down, both legs across the edge of the fire,
sending sparks and red-hot embers flying in all directions.

He was up again quicker than a scalded cat and went tearing round the tent, shaking the burning ashes from his trousers. A strong smell of singeing filled the air as the gypsy beat at his legs frantically with his bare hands. His clothes were not on fire, but he was badly scorched and shaken and almost immediately left the tent, his companions following him, without a word, into the black, rainy evening.

Seriously alarmed, Titch and Michael turned to find Patch Cooper doubled up and helpless, choking with laughter. Shocked, they stared at him; watched his shoulders quiver while his hands clutched at his knees. Little snorts and gurgles came from him and their faces began gradually to relax. After all, the fellow wasn't badly hurt, though he might well have been, and he *had* looked rather funny, careering round the tent, slapping himself as if attacked by a swarm of hungry mosquitoes. Titch and Michael, feeling rather guilty, allowed themselves a slow smile and waited for the little gypsy to raise his head.

"Bother," exclaimed Titch, propping his bicycle against his knee and searching in all his pockets. "I've lost my penknife. What can I have done with it? You haven't borrowed it, have you?" He had been repairing Michael's saddle-bag, which had burst under the strain and let loose a shower of belongings on to the road.

Michael shook his head. "I know what's happened," he said. "It slipped out of your shorts last night, when you were doing that handstand."

Titch snapped his fingers. "Of course!" he exclaimed. "I suppose it's no use going back, now. I might find it."

Michael looked down the road behind them. The first houses of Dalehurst showed not far ahead; cheerful and sunlit. The morning sky was blue; the sun already as warm on their backs as Patch Cooper had prophesied. Another five minutes and they would probably be seeing Crusoe. It seemed a pity to go all the way back, just for a penknife that might or might not be there. But from the tone of his brother's voice, he knew that Titch wanted to try.

"If you don't mind, I'll stay here," he said, thinking of his ankle, which was slightly swollen and still rather painful. "You go back. You can leave the tent and make yourself lighter. I'll look after everything."

Titch jumped at the idea. "Won't take me long. I should like to have a shot for it, though one of the gypsies is sure to have picked it up."

He was off and pedalling down the road before Michael had settled himself comfortably by the wayside. A gate made a suitable back, and he spread his mackintosh cape before sitting down, for the grass was still heavy with the night's rain. The sun shone mistily warm, transforming the countryside. Michael could hardly believe that this same, friendly-looking forest, now spreading in soft browny, blue-grey folds beyond the bright green fields, could have frowned so blackly under the low clouds yesterday evening. Then everything had been dark; painted in shades of darkness from black to grey; depressing and hostile; driving them to seek shelter and cheerful firelight in Patch Cooper's *lue*. But now all was gay with colour; the morning beckoned and they had left the frowsty, smoke-black interior of the tent to wash themselves in the cold, first sunlight; rays shining flatly across a meadow so pearled with dew and rain that the grass had looked like a shallow lake; gleaming and white and clean. The camp had been astir early, and they had woken to the noise of bumps and bangings; shouts, the neigh of horses, barking of dogs. It had taken them back to the circus, last summer, when the whole procession of lorries and horse-boxes had moved off each morning with the first glimmerings of dawn.

Patch Cooper had made them as comfortable as he could, and they had slept tight in the cosy atmosphere of the huge tent. They had been tired and only too ready for bed after the evening meal; even for a bed of sacks and straw with an old blanket to cover them, which was all he had been able to offer. Supper had been good, too! Whatever it was that the little gypsy had fished out of his fragrant-smelling, black pot, it had tasted exceedingly good. Eaten piping hot, with second and third helpings heaped on to their tin plates, and great hunks of bread and cheese to follow, they had glowed with warmth; filled with the feeling of good fellowship that comes when hunger is satisfied. Patch Cooper had talked to them, and sitting round the fire listening, not always understanding exactly what he meant because he used so many strange words, they learnt a great deal and soon began to feel that gypsies were not, after all, an alien people, impossible to know. While he spoke to them, crouched into a ball on his low stool, the flames licked up around the logs; firelight danced and flickered, filling the canvas dome with uncertain, wavering light, and behind his voice they heard always the persistent undertone of the steadily falling rain; rain slanting down, now hard, now soft, as the wind pressed the walls of the tent; rain filling the pitch black night outside with sound and driving wetness.

Michael leant back against the bars of the gate, eyes half-closed, still drowsy, thinking it all over. The dancing; the gymnastics that had followed; Patch Cooper's merriment; he recalled them all in turn. From some remark let fall, casually, the brothers gathered that Levi Ayres, the champion dancer, and his cronies, were not too popular with the older gypsies. In fact, the camp was rapidly splitting into two factions. "There's them as likes to stick at nothing, and them as won't gladly go agin the law o' the land," Patch Cooper had said to them. "As there's always them that's rougher than others. We've a few young fellows along of us who'll be running into trouble, I'm afeard." Michael had wondered what sort of trouble, but the gypsy had said no more on the subject, swinging the pot from the fire and drawing across the hamper full of plates and knives and cooking things.

And where were they all now? Michael turned his head idly, to look down the road. Along there, heading in the opposite direction; strung along the road, some in light carts, rod tents loaded aboard; others in small waggons—for it was summer now and they were off on the move again, making their way down to the sea coast. Before they had started, he had watched them complete the destruction of Urania Pinfold's waggon; throwing the metal parts, including the heavy stove, into a muddy pool close by. Now only a black scar on the meadow showed where the funeral pyre had taken place, and as the summer progressed, fresh green grass would spring up from the ashes and cover all trace of the fire.

How long had Titch been gone? Michael began to keep a look out, hoping to see him reappear round the bend at the bottom of the hill. Several tradesmen's vans had passed, coming out from Dalehurst, and a private car or two. He watched a pony trap climb towards him; a smart outfit that attracted his attention, for he thought it might belong to one of the gypsies. But the very respectable, large woman driving the cob was certainly not one of them, and Michael, glancing away as she passed, saw a cyclist come into view at the foot of the slope. At last; here was Titch! Now they would soon be started again.

But Titch wore no very cheerful expression, and flopped down with a grunt on a corner of Michael's cape, breathing deeply, for he had pedalled all the way up the hill. "No luck," he said. "I looked everywhere, too. I saw some people, they might have taken it, but they were too far away for me to shout."

"What sort of people?" Michael inquired.

"Oh, a couple of kids pushing a pram," said Titch off-handedly.

In silence, they fixed the tent and groundsheet and pushed their bicycles up to the crest of the slope. Below and behind them the forest spread, feathery dove-grey and brown; a tapestry of bare branches rising and falling with the gentle hills and valleys. Then the houses and shops of the small country town shut them in, and they mounted and pedalled through the crowded, busy little main street. Everybody seemed to be bustling about; shopping, gossiping, walking with full baskets. They passed by the church; the road began to slope down again and they free-wheeled along between the houses. Quite soon they came out of the town and saw the forest again, not below them this time, but straight ahead and very close. Round a bend a wide green space opened out, and as Patch Cooper had said, there was the white building on the left, with a sign hanging over the door; a large,

painted tree with the name in big letters underneath;
The Royal Oak. And there, across by the forest's edge,
standing on a level patch of grass, was the caravan;
paintwork fresh and shining; a thin column of smoke
rising from the black stump of chimney projecting from
the roof.

"*Crusoe!*" bawled Titch, waking the echoes.

The chestnut horse, grazing close by, tossed up his
head, startled. Then the waggon door jerked open and a
tall, thin figure appeared on the top step, stooping under
the carved porch. With a wave of his hand he jumped to
the ground and came bounding across the green to
meet them.

"Looks just the same!" Michael said, half aloud,
noticing Crusoe's brightly coloured shirt open at the
neck, sleeves rolled up above his elbows, grey flannel
trousers securely hitched with a thick leather belt. He
smiled to himself, remembering the summer before and
the things that had happened to them, then. Their
adventures had started early, this time, but they'd
arrived safe and sound; they had found his camp and
here he was, just the same as ever, with his horse and
caravan. Things slipped back into place; everything
would now continue as before. And holidays, he thought,
as they exchanged greetings and walked together, pushing
their bicycles across the grass—holidays with Crusoe were
never very likely to be dull!

CHAPTER 7

Goods to Deliver

"WELL, I don't know!" said Derek, pausing for breath. "He may be with them, he may not. But it's funny the Crosbies being there. Crusoe said they might be coming, in his letter. Remember?"

The muddy track sloped steeply between the hazels and birches, and both Derek and Diana needed all their strength to push Cynthia's chair up the hill. They slithered and slipped, and at every short rest they continued the same endless discussion. Where was Crusoe?

"I'm sure he wouldn't have left the Royal Oak," Diana seemed to think. "After all, he knows we're coming."

"Doesn't expect us as soon as this," Derek reminded her. "And you'd think they'd stick together, wouldn't you? I mean, why should the Crosbies go off with the gypsies all by themselves? Besides," he added in a tone which clinched the matter, "they don't *know* anything about them. Crusoe must be there, too."

And Diana had to admit the logic of his reasoning.

"*I* think," said Cynthia, as brother and sister began to push and heave the chair through the sticky, slippery mud, "that you'd better stop arguing and ask Daddy when we get home."

Derek frowned. He waited until they reached a level stretch before he answered her.

"You seem to forget that we're still Philip and Margaret . . ." he began, but Cynthia interrupted him. Sitting quietly, she had plenty of breath to spare for quick talking.

"That's silly," she said. "You can easily find out what you want to know, without giving anything away. You can if you're clever enough."

"Why don't you ask him, then?" replied Derek with some heat.

"All right, I will, if you're afraid."

"I'm not afraid. I don't really mind asking him. P'raps he'll know where the gypsies have gone to."

"I can tell you *that!*" said Cynthia. "They're going to the seaside."

Derek and Diana looked at each other, surprised. Gypsies by the sea? Surely not? The idea seemed too fanciful to be true.

"Are you sure you're not thinking of nigger minstrels?" asked Derek, but Cynthia didn't take it as a joke.

"You needn't believe me," she flashed. "I hope you never do find your friends, that's all."

"Sorry," Derek mumbled. "You're probably right. Just seems a bit queer to me. I've never seen gypsies anywhere near the seaside."

"But Derek, we can't go right down to the coast. Why that's miles and miles."

"We needn't go all the way," said Derek. "We'll try to catch them up. Start as soon as we get back. We can hitch-hike again or take a bus."

"But do find out for certain. I'm sure he wouldn't go all that far away." Diana was still holding fast to Crusoe's telegram. The Royal Oak, he'd said. How could he expect them to follow him down to the sea?

"D'you think Mrs. Potts would drive us part of the way?" Derek asked Cynthia. He, for his part, was busily forming plans. Vaguely, at the back of his mind, glittered a wide, restless expanse of moving water, burnished by the sun. He pictured the gypsies camped high on a cliff; Crusoe and Titch and Michael sleeping with them to the muffled tread of the breakers. Already the sea was a magnet, drawing him out of the forest.

Impatiently, he pressed forward; the track was drier up here; the going a great deal easier. They came out on to the road again—and in five minutes arrived back at Cynthia's home. They were only to find, however, that Mrs. Potts had driven into Dalehurst and was not expected to return for another hour at least.

The gardener's boy told them where she was; holding open the gate for Derek as he pushed the chair round to the french windows of the drawing-room, opening on to the lawn. He was a red-faced, cheery youth with a shock of hair as pale as bleached straw.

"Company for dinner!" he said, giving Cynthia a knowing grin before he retired to the far end of the garden.

"Bother!" said Cynthia absently. "Can you move me round a bit, I want to look *that* way."

Derek settled her and then turned to go indoors. "Coming?" he asked his sister.

"What are you going to do?"

"Pack," said Derek briefly.

"But you're not leaving *now!*" cried Cynthia. "Aren't you going to wait for Potty? And you haven't asked Daddy about . . ."

Just at that moment, Mr. Crawley came through the open windows and joined them on the lawn outside.

"I was wondering where you'd hidden yourselves," he said, cheerily. "I'd like a little assistance from you, Philip, if you please. By the way," he added, "the Finsbury-Jones are coming along to see us. You'll re-

member they met you last year, at Swanage I think it
was. You were staying at the same hotel. They knew all
about you as soon as I mentioned your names."

"Oh yes," stuttered Derek. "Yes, of course." And with
a backward glance at the others he followed Mr. Crawley
into the house.

Diana stared after him; horrorstruck. Even Cynthia
was taken by surprise and seemed at a loss for words.

"You'll have to go, quickly," she said at last. "Before
lunch."

"Yes, but how? Where?" Diana sounded quite
desperate. "We can't just walk out. Someone might
see us."

Cynthia sat, hand on her chin, thinking. After a while
she looked up and gazed across the garden to the distant
figure working on one of the flower beds.

"There's always Albert," she said, and putting her
fingers in her mouth she blew a shrill whistle. The flaxen
head jerked up; tools were dropped, and the gardener's
boy came striding quickly towards them across the
grass.

"He looks after the pony," Cynthia explained in an
undertone. "Often drives and fetches things when Mrs.
Potts is busy. I'm beginning to think of something . . ."

An earnest conversation ensued. The grin on the rosy,
round face grew wider; the head of bleached straw
nodded vigorously. Now and then Diana put in a sugges-
tion, and Albert punctuated proceedings with a steady
"Yes, Miss" that never varied. Apart from these slight
interruptions Cynthia did all the talking; leaning forward
in her chair, thin face framed in red curls, gazing up
earnestly as she repeated her instructions.

Derek reappeared just as Albert had been given leave

to depart. Cynthia and Diana pounced on him. Had he found out anything? Was Crusoe with the gypsies?

"Your father saw Titch and Michael," said Derek, looking a little worried. "He had a talk with Titch, and stopped a fight between him and one of the gypsies. There was a fire, I couldn't quite follow what he meant. But he didn't actually see Crusoe . . ."

"Does he think he's with them?"

"Well—no," Derek was forced to admit. "But of course he can't be quite certain. I couldn't very well ask him directly; it was a bit difficult. I wish we knew . . ."

"Derek, I'm *sure* he's at the Royal Oak. I'm not going to try and follow the gypsies." Diana's face was firmly set.

Her brother hesitated. "You won't . . ."

Cynthia interrupted them. "That's settled then," she said. "Albert'll drive you to the Forest Road, as soon as Potty comes back."

"And if he isn't there?"

"Well, then, we *will* go to the sea," Diana replied, clinching the issue.

Derek reluctantly agreed that this was the best plan.

"But how . . ." he started to ask.

Diana took his arm. "Cynthia's arranged everything," she said. "You come upstairs with me and I'll explain. I bet you'll think it's a jolly good scheme."

"I don't know so much," grunted Derek a few minutes later. He was leaning out of his bedroom window, letting down a large and heavy bundle on the end of a length of rope; their rucksacks and mackintoshes. "Seems a lot of trouble to me. I'd just walk out and risk it. Someone will have to explain us, sooner or later."

The baggage reached ground and Derek tossed the rope after it. A fair-haired boy emerged from the stable across

D

the paved yard and gathered up the pile; vanishing through the same doorway from which he had come. A moment after they heard the sound of hooves; the crunch of wheels on the gravel of the drive.

"Just in time," breathed Diana, as they retreated from the open window. "She's back quicker than they thought. Now we'll soon be off. Let's go and say good-bye to Cynthia."

They marched downstairs and through the drawing-room. Cynthia, back twisted round, was waiting impatiently for them.

"Potty's come," she said in an urgent whisper. "I *must* see you go away. Wheel me through to the front of the house, *quickly*."

Derek pushed her chair through the french windows; manœuvred skilfully between the settee and the piano, and came out into the hall at a rapid trot. They heard the sound of voices; saw strange people through the glass panels ahead, standing in the porch. The front door opened; the visitors were almost upon them—and at the same moment the latch of Mr. Crawley's study door clicked and Cynthia's father came striding up the passage, cutting off their escape. This was it, thought Derek, checking his stride. Mrs. Potts must have brought the guests back with her, in the pony trap. She was ushering them into the house; they were face to face with them and there was no way out. But he had not reckoned on Cynthia's presence of mind.

"Through that door," she said in a rapid undertone. "Leave me here and run for it. Go downstairs and out by the kitchen."

Derek and Diana needed no second bidding. They were through the door in a flash, almost tumbling down the short flight of stairs. Somebody was clattering pots and pans; a rich smell of cooking greeted them; they paused for a moment and then——

"This way!" Derek gasped, and they were outside the house and running across to the stables. Albert stepped from the shadows and greeted them with the solemn face of a fellow-conspirator. Straw rustled under their feet, and the air was warm and smelt of a mixture of horse and hay. . . .

"Yes, I'm very well," Cynthia was saying. "Yes, quite, thank you. No, I haven't yet. I say, could you push me out on to the porch? I wanted to watch . . . the pony . . ."

"Now don't start giving way to her, Mrs. Jones," grumbled Cynthia's guardian angel. "I'm always after her. She gives a body no peace, but it's always 'move me here, move me there.' 'Tisn't as if she couldn't be independent. She could use her crutches, but bless me, they don't suit her ladyship."

"Oh, Potty, don't be beastly; I'll put on my irons after lunch, I will really. Just move me this once."

"You'll catch cold, sitting out there in a draught."

"Only for a *minute*," Cynthia pleaded. "Potty, *do!*"

As the front door was opened, and Mrs. Potts, with a great deal more grumbling, pushed her chair out on to the porch, they heard the clatter of hooves in the yard, and pony and trap came round the side of the house; Albert sitting, proudly erect, on the wooden seat. Behind him, Cynthia noted with sparkling eyes two round, sack-covered bundles. Mrs. Potts stared down curiously from the top step.

"Where's he a'going to?" she demanded. "What's he got in the cart there?"

"Oh, some things to deliver," said Cynthia airily.

Mrs. Potts caught her eye and then, holding her sides, began to quiver very gently. Behind them, Mr. Crawley was conducting Mr. and Mrs. Finsbury-Jones through into the drawing-room. His precise, courteous voice could be heard, commenting upon the pleasant change in the weather. Mrs. Potts slowly shook her head from side to side.

"You are a one," she said. "You are a one!"

But Derek, smothered and choked in the pitch blackness under the sacks, felt that such an indignity was the very last straw. Give a girl her head and this sort of thing was the result! Why, they could have got away a hundred times more comfortably by themselves, without all this ridiculous fuss and palaver. He would never have hidden under his sack if Diana hadn't insisted on it. He was hot and dusty and his nose tickled; he wanted to sneeze and he could scarcely draw breath. The floorboards were hard; the trap jolted and jarred his knees; he had a crick in his neck and his back ached. Derek was about to sum up his discomforts and find a really satisfactory expression for them, when the covering was plucked from his head and he popped up into a rush of light and air like a swimmer surfacing after a deep, deep dive. He looked up, startled, into the grinning, rosy face of the gardener's boy, and found they were out in open country and had made good their escape.

"You don't 'arf look a sight!" was Albert's greeting, as he reached across and pulled Diana's sack away. She emerged, wide-eyed and strangely pale. At the sight of her pallid face, dusted with flour, Albert nearly fell off the narrow seat, and the cob went zig-zagging down the road, startled by his sudden guffaw. Derek was not amused. He wiped his face with his handkerchief, and tousled his hair vigorously. A cloud of white dust filled the air.

"I think you might have chosen clean sacks," he said.

Back at the Crawley's, the gong had sounded for lunch.

"And where are Philip and Margaret?" inquired Mrs. Finsbury-Jones as they sat themselves down at the dining-room table. "Didn't you tell me . . ."

"I'm afraid they couldn't be prevailed upon to stay indoors," Mr. Crawley replied. "They had some plan of their own. An excursion was it, Cynthia? A picnic in the forest? We don't expect to see them again until this evening." His face was quite serious as he gazed across at his daughter.

Mrs. Potts, handing round the vegetables, went brick-red and, in her flurry, very nearly dropped the dish on to the carpet. Cynthia stared at her father, open-mouthed. So he knew, then! He'd found out!

"They were very sorry indeed to have missed you," Mr. Crawley added, turning to his guests. "But you know what it is, when children get an idea into their heads. There's just no stopping them!"

CHAPTER 8

Forest Trail

"GOOD-BYE!" called Diana as Albert turned the cob. "Thanks for bringing us," and Derek, who had forgotten about the flour sacks, gave him a cheery wave of his hand. Then, as pony and trap and flaxen-haired driver clip-clopped smartly down the Forest Road, brother and sister followed the rough, muddy track leading into the trees; the track that was to bring them to the Royal Oak and Crusoe.

"I'm glad we didn't come here in the dark, last night," said Derek, as they slithered and stumbled forward. "It's even muddier than the lane to the clearing!"

"I wonder why it's so rutted." Diana was picking her way fastidiously between the pools of rainwater. "Horses and carts must come along this way. Where d'you think they go to?"

Derek had no idea. "There's no farm or anything marked on the map," he said. "Nothing but forest."

The sun shone brilliantly; they were even grateful for the shade of the tree-trunks and the high, interlacing branches. Looking up, the sky seemed a deeper blue than they had ever known it, and every branch and twig was golden in the light.

"It *is* a lovely day," Diana sighed. "We're getting quite deep into the forest now, aren't we? Did you hear that woodpecker? They are funny when they laugh!"

They stopped to listen, but the yaffle did not repeat his mocking call. The primroses and anemones growing at the side of the path reminded her of their morning's walk with Cynthia.

"I wish we needn't have left her," she said. "Rushing off like that. I say, Derek!" An idea had struck her. "D'you think Crusoe would mind. . . . Could we . . ." She splashed into a puddle and the brown water wetted her ankle and filled her shoe. "Could we ask him if we might—I'm sure he wouldn't mind!"

Derek waited patiently, but Diana was so full of the idea that she forgot to make herself plain and rushed on.

"It would be good for her, don't you think so? To be with all of us, and we'd do things together and not take any notice. I think that's what she needs, most of all."

"You mean, Cynthia, to come with us and Crusoe? Camping out?" Derek whistled. "Bit of a tall order I should say, but I suppose it *could* be done. What about her cousins, anyway? They're arriving to-day. The real ones." And Derek grinned; wondering how different they would be. What a shock Mr. Crawley would get when he saw them arrive!

Diana had forgotten Philip and Margaret. "After they've gone, perhaps. I'll ask Crusoe. D'you think we could have lunch soon," she added, "I'm getting really hungry and Albert said he'd scrounged a nice lot for us. Honestly you know, she thought of everything." And Derek had to admit that Cynthia had shown all the qualities of good generalship.

They sat themselves down under a beech-tree and rested back against the smooth trunk. The roots made a convenient seat for each of them, and looking up, the tree became a vast, grey-green pillar bursting into a feathery maze right at the very summit.

Derek opened his rucksack; dragged out a large, white paper bag and peered eagerly inside. "Sausage rolls!" he called, and searched in his luggage again. "Cake!" he said, coming up with another packet. "Apples! Biscuits! He's done us proud!"

And without more ado they started to tuck in.

"How much farther have we got to go?" Diana asked him as they arrived at the apple stage. Derek was folding the odd scraps of paper and putting them back into his rucksack; he was a naturally tidy person.

"About a mile, I should think. Depends how straight the path is."

"How will you know the way?"

"We've got to keep going straight ahead," said Derek, getting up. "If we meet anyone, I'll ask, of course."

"Not much chance of that," Diana seemed to think, as they swung on their rucksacks and set off again.

They kept up as good a pace as they were able, but the ground was soft and the going tired them. The trees in this part of the forest, oaks, ashes and beeches, were all bare; buds still hard; no sign yet of an unfurling leaf. An occasional holly made a clump of dark, solid colour; otherwise the grey and moss-green trunks and branches, patterned in a net of fine shadows, spread openly in every direction. All was light and airy; warm under the blue sky. Then at last they reached a barrier of tall firs, and the track led them to a gate on which they leaned, and surveyed their route to come.

Straight as a die, the ride ahead was cut between the cliff-like sides of the great trees. On either hand, nothing but closed ranks of silent, tapering trunks; even as candles; row upon row upon row. No green grass in there; no flowers carpeting the ground; only a rust-brown covering of withered needles receding into the dense gloom.

"I don't like it so much," said Diana. "This isn't a proper forest. Why it's a plantation!"

"I expect we'll come out again into the forest, on the other side," said Derek. "We must carry straight ahead, that's certain."

They opened the gate and walked on, inhaling the piney scent of resin. The sky was a narrow slit above them; the dark, silent plantations brooded on either side.

"Trees are smaller, farther along," said Derek presently, and after a while, as if the forest roof were fashioned in a series of great steps, they found the trees smaller still. The track was no longer a cleft between sheer precipices; the arch of blue broadened over them and they felt the sun again.

"Planted in different years, I expect," said Derek. "Don't they grow them close together? The bigger ones were much farther apart. These would do fine for Christmas trees, wouldn't they?"

"Somebody's working," Diana caught the sound of voices. "Foresters, I expect. Oh, Derek, look—they're planting!"

Beyond the smallest trees, scarcely as tall as they were, they saw the stooping figures of men; heard the clink and crunch of a spade. They hesitated; wondering whether they ought to continue; whether the foresters would mind them passing through the plantations. But after a short pause, they walked on into the clearing. Already, half the open space was covered with rows of tiny trees; minute replicas of the giant firs rising away behind them at the forest edge. The whole area, like the plantations of smaller trees they had just passed, was bounded with

D*

wire netting. Inside the wire, four men were working.
Only one of them noticed their approach, and he nodded
his head cheerily enough as Derek and Diana drew
slowly closer and then stopped to watch.

Down went the spade, and the ground was prised
open just wide enough to admit the young tree's roots.
In went the sapling; the spade was withdrawn; the earth
pressed around the small stem, and the planters passed
on to the next tree. As quickly as that they moved along
their line, and meanwhile the other men were preparing
the row to come; working with stretched cord and a
measuring rod. At even distances across the clearing, the
woodman lifted one of the little saplings from the pouch
hung in front of him and laid it on the ground, ready
for the planters. They did not hurry; neither did they
pause, and the ranks of newly-planted trees stood to
attention behind them, their numbers always swelling,
testifying to a good day's work.

The man with a piece of sacking draped round his
middle—he looked like a mother kangaroo, thought
Diana—had finished laying down his row, and they
watched while the cord was moved sideways into position
for a new line. One of the men was quite close to them
now. Derek plucked up courage, advanced a step or two,
and asked him the way.

"The Royal Oak?" repeated the woodman, and the
wrinkles shot up on his brown, weatherbeaten forehead as
he unbent himself. He put two fingers under the peak of
his cloth cap and scratched his hair. "By right's you
shouldn't be coming down here, but I reckon you can
find your way through. Did you turn in from the Forest
Road?"

Derek nodded.

"Ah, there's many who make the mistake. You should have followed the track 'bout quarter mile farther down the road. I'll tell you what." The woodman turned, tilted back his cap and pointed a brawny arm; shirt sleeve rolled up to the elbow. "Go along here," he said, "and turn to the right when you come to the larches. You'll have to pass through the Nurseries. You'll find a gate at the far end. Bear left-ish, not sharp left mind, and you'll come to the oak."

"About how far?" asked Derek, and the woodman, scratching his head again, reckoned it would take them a good half hour. They thanked him, and with a last backward glance at the neat rows of little fir-trees, strode off again along the track.

"What did he say?" panted Diana, for Derek was setting a furious pace. "Through the Nurseries?"

"Where they grow all the seedlings, I suppose," said Derek. "What a nuisance, not being on the right track. It's a much more difficult place to find than I'd ever thought. The map doesn't show another way through; it doesn't even mark all these plantations. Just says 'forest.' I don't think it can be a very good one."

"I wonder Albert didn't know. He started us off wrong," said Diana, but Derek seemed to think that the map was more to blame than the gardener's boy.

"Here are the larches," he said at last, as the tall spires rose in front of them. A haze of delicate green filmed the trees; brilliant in the afternoon sunshine.

"Much nicer than firs," Diana thought aloud. "They're so black and dull. I don't like trees to be always the same."

The main track bent to the right and at the far end they could see the shapes of low buildings. They plodded on; past an open space where the trees had recently been felled. The pale discs of stumps, sawn across close above their roots, studded the ground and piles of brushwood and small branches were stacked neatly at intervals.

"No wonder the track's rutted," said Derek. "They must cart all the timber this way, out to the road."

"D'you think we'll see a team, Derek?" Diana asked eagerly.

Derek shook his head. "Shouldn't think so," he said. "That's a winter job. Good fun, to watch them felling!" And he crossed to one of the sawn stumps and squatted over it, counting the rings. "Fifty-seven," he announced after a pause. "Though I may have missed one or two, where they've chopped the bark with an axe."

Diana looked down at the smooth, clean-cut wood. "Would these trees have been as big as the first ones? The firs, right at the edge? I suppose they'll cut them down next winter."

Derek agreed that they probably would. "Planting time, now," he said. "But I'd like to see them fell some really big trees. Much more exciting."

"Derek, just think how long they've got to wait!" Diana had suddenly realized, more clearly than ever before, the huge gap between seed-time and harvest, when trees, not corn or vegetables, was the crop. "These trees were sixty years old, about. And pines and firs are the quickest growers, aren't they? I know oaks are hundreds of years old. Well, even if a man spent all his life working in the same forest, he would only *just* be able to cut down a tree he had planted himself."

Derek calculated rapidly. "That's right," he said. "But felling is much too tough a job for an old man, anyway. I don't expect they ever do."

"So they're always planting for other people, and reaping other people's work?"

"Don't suppose it makes any difference—one fir's very like another," said Derek, but Diana was away and lost in a daydream. What was it she had been reading about quite recently, that the work of these foresters recalled? The life of the men who, hundreds of years ago, had started to build a cathedral. That was it! Men who had no hope of ever seeing their task completed and brought to a final conclusion. Men who knew that the next generation, perhaps even the generation after that, would reap where they had sown; complete the building whose foundations they had helped to dig. She looked across the clearing to the tall trunks lining the far side; rising cool and grey in their even rows. The sun slanted down through the thick boughs, finding a crevice here, a crack there, through which to poke a narrow, golden beam and touch to brilliance one dusty corner of the softly needled floor. In there everything was hushed; remote from any stir of wind. . . .

"Come along," called the impatient Derek. "What are you dreaming about now?"

"Cathedrals," said Diana abruptly and, giving her rucksack a hitch, she followed her brother up the muddy track.

The Nurseries were small paddocks all carefully fenced and wired against rabbits; sheltered by the plantations and criss-crossed with small paths. More foresters were at work there, and they looked up as Derek and Diana walked by. One of them called out and Derek stopped to answer him. When he heard that they had already spoken to the men back in the plantations, the forester seemed satisfied and let them continue.

He was digging a narrow trench through the black, well-sifted earth, and before moving on Diana saw his fellow-worker lift a long double board and place it over the slit he had made in the ground. Between the planks were gripped the heads of the seedlings; their roots dangled out and fitted into the trench. Earth was shovelled in; the boards hinged at the top, were opened and removed, and there was the row of little green plants all set firm in the ground; planted close together in a straight line.

"That must save some time," said Derek as they passed. "Isn't everything neat and tidy." True enough, the carpet of tiny seedlings; planted with mathematical precision, were as spick and span and weedless as the most careful gardener could desire.

The track skirted the low sheds and outbuildings and ahead of them they saw the gate. The fir-trees stopped as abruptly as they had begun and beyond them they caught a glimpse of the real forest.

"There you are! Now we're getting somewhere." Derek sounded quite relieved. "Bear leftish, the man said. Not sharp left."

They passed through the gate and the track they had followed for so long petered out into a series of small footpaths, leading off in every possible direction. Derek tried to follow the woodman's instructions and, after some hesitation, chose his path.

"I only hope it's the right one," he said.

Above them, drifting steadily across the sky, were several flakes of white cloud; soft and delicate as thistle-down. Behind them came others; islands floating in a lake of blue. Lower still in the sky, but rising all the time, a flat, grey cloud-continent slowly heaved itself, without a

break or gap as far as the eye could see. At that moment,
the first outlying fragment touched the sun and a cool
breeze came with the shadow.

"We've had the best of the day," said Diana, looking
up. "Never mind. Not so long now before we'll be with
Crusoe."

They walked on steadily; the path was drier and
smoother than the rutted track and they made good
progress. Every now and then they came to a fork or a
crossing and Derek had to choose which track to follow.
As they went farther into the forest, and turning back,
could no longer see the dark wall of the fir plantations
behind them, Diana began to look anxiously about for land-
marks. There were not many things to hold on to, in this
sort of wood; fewer than you would think. Here was an
old oak, limbs spreading out sideways, a loop of ivy
trailed over the mossy trunk. Just beyond, on the other
side of a patch of dry, brown bracken, grew a skimpy
holly bush. Then a bramble clump; a smaller tree;
another oak similar in size and shape to the last, and yet
another holly bush. Only here and there did they pass
something strikingly different; a great bough torn off
and hanging from it's splintered end; a fallen tree
bridging a ditch full of muddy water. These few things
she could be certain of recognizing again, should the
need arise. And you never could tell! Derek, she felt,
was trusting more to luck than to good judgment, and
one tree, however large, was a very, very small point in
all this boundless forest.

"How long d'you think we've been walking?" he said
at last. Derek, too, had been keeping a sharp look out;
but he was watching all the time for a tree much larger
than it's fellows. He was anticipating the giant bulk of

the Royal Oak, and had no eyes for the small fry they were passing through. These oaks here, he thought, were as minnows to a trout. They would come to the older, bigger trees before very long; he was sure of that.

"Half an hour, *quite*," said Diana.

"We stopped in the plantation, don't forget. We're bound to think we've been walking longer than we really have. I'm not worrying yet," Derek said cheerily.

Very soon the character of the forest changed; the trees were becoming bigger! They passed down a grassy ride between tall beeches; always on the watch for the flash of bright paintwork that would tell them they were near their goal. Now they were entering an oak wood; there was a very large tree over on the far side, thought Derek. The trunk was squat and vast; only a few huge boughs remained, but each was as thick as the trunk of a normal tree. Where was the *Guide!* Better have a look at the picture and make quite sure. He pulled the strap from his left shoulder when he recollected himself. No need, of course. If it was the tree they wanted, Crusoe would be there. Perhaps on the other side they would see the caravan.

They caught no glimpse of a waggon, but as they approached, the tree seemed to grow more and more immense. It towered in front of them; a bastion of rough bark as wide as a haystack. Could there possibly be two trees this size, Derek wondered. And the shape? The way that limb shot out at an angle, like a policeman holding up the traffic. He *must* have a look at the photograph!

But as he fumbled in his rucksack, trying to find the little guide book, Diana suddenly called out. She had walked on round the tree; passing him as he stopped to investigate.

"What?" he shouted, thinking she must have seen the caravan. "Is he there?"

"Derek, I've found a board," she cried, running back to him. "This is it. It says so. This is the Royal Oak."

"And Crusoe?"

Derek scarcely needed an answer to *that* question. Slowly he pulled the cord of his rucksack tight and tied a neat bow. Leisurely, he fastened the buckle on the flap. The discovery had come in such a matter-of-fact way that he had not yet fully grasped how serious it was. Crusoe not here, Crusoe not at the Royal Oak. . . . He met Diana's gaze and stood up, still moving very slowly, as if he had some hours of time before him and nothing whatever to do.

"Well," he said, holding the rucksack strap loosely in his fingers. "What now?"

And from somewhere far away in the silent forest a woodpecker mocked at them, and was quiet again.

CHAPTER 9

Afraid of the Dark?

"No sign of any camp. I'm sure we'd see the marks," said Derek, moving around. "He obviously hasn't been here. I know what happened!" he exclaimed, turning to his sister. "He must have decided to go off with the gypsies *after* he'd told us about the Royal Oak, and I bet you he's sent us another wire! He didn't expect us to leave home till to-morrow. We should have waited, really; then we'd know where to meet him."

"What d'you think we'd better do?" asked Diana. "Go back into Dalehurst and telephone? Mummy will have opened the telegram."

"Yes, we could . . ." Derek hesitated. "But we know he's with the gypsies, now, and they've gone down to the sea. We might catch them up if we were lucky and got a lift at once. Anyway, first thing to do is to get back to the plantations and through on to the road again." He walked across to his rucksack and swung it on to his shoulders. "Wish I had a watch," he muttered. "I suppose it must be three o'clock, at least. Still, we've got plenty of time."

They began to walk back along the green grass path between the dead bracken and bramble thickets. At the first division of the ways Derek paused, looking around him.

"We should have marked the trail as we came along," he said.

"We didn't think we'd be coming back," said Diana feelingly."

"Never mind, we can't go far wrong. We know the direction and that's the main thing. The sun . . ." And Derek looked up, but the flat greyness had spread and covered the whole sky and the sun had disappeared.

"I think we came by that tree over there," said Diana, after another five minutes.

"Derek, we never passed this stream," she declared, a few minutes later. They both stood on the little bridge, so thickly covered with grass as to have become part of the track itself. The water gurgled merrily and ran a ceaseless tongue up the side of a half-submerged log, black and shiny as a hippopotamus.

"Just a little farther this way," said Derek. "Then we'll try and work to the left. We'll probably find a path going in the direction we want."

"I wonder who built that bracken hut?" Diana asked, as they came out into a clearing where four or five paths met. Derek was too busy checking up on his direction to pay her much attention.

"Down here, I should say. Perhaps we *were* going too much . . . Oh, foresters, I expect." He glanced at the little erection in the corner of the glade; a framework of poles with walls of tightly packed bracken. "Looks easy enough to make." He did not go across to investigate, but led off along the track he had chosen, and Diana, with a backward glance, followed a little wearily after him.

They walked for another ten minutes and then she demanded a rest. They sat down, with their rucksacks beside them, on the driest patch of ground they could find. The forest was very grey now; the trees as grey as the sky. Tree after tree spreading away into a misty greyness.

"What else have we got to eat?" she asked. "I'm

hungry again already. And thirsty. I wish we'd kept those apples."

Derek rummaged, without much success. All he could produce was a small packet of chocolate.

"Make me thirstier than ever," said Diana, refusing the piece he broke off for her.

Derek munched his share in silence and carefully returned the rest of the packet. When they set off again, their rucksacks did not weigh any lighter and their feet had a heavy, leaden feel; their muscles no longer springy and elastic.

"We should be coming to the plantations, by this time," said Diana.

"We can't very well miss them," said Derek reassuringly. "They stretch for miles. We shall know where we are then, even if we don't hit the gate by the nurseries."

They searched the forest ahead for a hint of the black, even line of fir-trees between the grey-green, lichen-covered trunks of the oaks, the ashes, and the hornbeams; the clumps and clusters of hazels and silver birches. They began to long for a sight of the ordered layout of the plantations; anything rather than this haphazard, straggling, ivy- and bramble-clad, leafless forest that stretched, grey and interminable, in every direction around them. They saw a magpie, flying low, fluttering his long tail between the branches; a rabbit scuttered across the path ahead; things unseen rustled in the bracken as they passed. Although so quiet, the forest was alive; everywhere animals and birds were living who belonged here, thought Diana; belonged as much as the trees. Only *they* were hurrying, hurrying, trying to get out; trying to get away. And the forest wouldn't let them go, but placed tree after tree after tree before them and laid a network of bewildering paths in front of their feet.

"We should get there soon," said Derek for the third time.

"We *must* be nearly there," he said, a short while later.

"No, of course I'm not lost," he said after another ten minutes had passed. "Don't be silly. I know perfectly well where we're going. This is the direction. We came . . ."

"Mind you," he said, pausing for Diana to catch him up. (How many hours had they been walking! How many endless, weary hours!) "I don't say we're going *directly* there. But we'll come out sooner or later, never you mind."

"Funny! Perhaps I went wrong, that last turning we took. If we'd followed on more to the right . . ."

"All the paths look so much the *same!*" said Derek, a note of irritation in his voice.

"Now I'm sure I've seen that tree before!" He brightened up again. "We must be right. Probably back on the path we came in by. I'm sure I remember that tree."

"Derek," said a little, cold voice behind him.

Derek turned and found his sister standing, stock still, in the middle of the open stretch of grass they had just skirted. "Come on!" he cried encouragingly. "I know where we are now."

"So do I," said Diana in the same flat voice.

"Good!" said Derek. "Want another rest? Not a bad idea. Feeling a bit fagged myself." And he retraced his steps, swinging off his rucksack as he came.

"What's the matter?" he asked as he reached her.

Diana had not moved; she seemed, indeed, to have lost the power of movement and, standing like a statue, repeated her remark in the same, cold, stony little voice, drained of all feeling.

"Hullo!" said Derek, following her gaze. "Another of those little bracken huts. Well, I suppose we might do worse, at a pinch!" He laughed, but as he glanced across the green clearing where four or five paths met, the familiarity of the scene suddenly broke in upon him. With a look of consternation, he turned and stared all round. "Why, we have—this is . . . It's the same hut!" he cried. "We went down there before and——"

"And came out here," said Diana, pointing to the track behind them. "We've gone in a circle." And she traced a wide sweep in the air with one of her hands.

Derek was quite dumbfounded. He gulped and stared again, unable to believe his eyes. "We can't!" he said at last. "Why, we've been walking for ages. We can't just be here. I know I was going straight on."

Diana shrugged her shoulders. "Let's have a rest, anyway," she decided, and Derek, after another look about him, followed her across the clearing to the bracken hut.

The shelter turned it's back towards them, the open side facing towards the trees, and it was with the slightest of pauses, an almost imperceptible hesitation, that Diana came round the corner. After all, a hut was a hut, and anybody *might* be asleep inside. But the three walls contained nothing more frightening than a pile of loose bracken.

"Just a minute," said Derek, who had caught her up. He pulled a length of stick out of a bramble bush and thoroughly beat about inside the shelter; tossing the brown, dry fronds into the air. "Don't want to go and sit on an adder," he explained briefly, and flung the branch away. "That's all right now." And brother and sister eased themselves of their rucksacks and stretched out gratefully in the snug interior.

Neither spoke for quite a few minutes. Derek was staring gloomily at the floor; lying on his tummy, face cupped in his hands.

"I'm sorry, Di," he said at last. "I've been an awful ass. You'd better lead, after this. I don't seem to be any good in a forest."

"I don't suppose I should do any better," said Diana. "I did think, well, sometimes, when you went one way I should have gone another, but I wouldn't dare . . . I don't think I'd like to try, even."

"You've probably got a bump of direction," Derek encouraged her. "Some people have. Like pigeons, and dogs—find their way home wherever they've been taken to."

Diana shook her head, unwilling to take on such a responsibility. "I'd rather not," she said. "I'll help you, if you like, but you lead."

"If only I had a compass," sighed Derek. "Honestly, there are dozens of things I want." He counted the months aloud. "Ages till my birthday, too. I want a watch and a compass and a really decent penknife and . . ."

"Can't you tell your direction any other way?"

"I can't," said Derek. "Not unless I can see the sun. Or the stars," he added. "I'm not much good at all the constellations, but I know the Great Bear and that's roughly north."

"What about the moss on tree trunks?" asked Diana. "I'm sure I read somewhere . . ."

Derek leapt to his feet. "Of course!" he cried. "Moss grows on the north side, away from the sun." And he plunged out into the wood.

Diana watched him going from one trunk to another; stamping down the brambles and bracken. He was gradually working his way deeper into the forest.

"Don't go too far," she called, and in another few minutes Derek returned, frowning and shaking his head.

"They're mossy all round," he said. "I think that dodge must work best in summer, in the very dry months. It's so sheltered and damp here, the moss just grows everywhere."

"Is it raining?" Diana asked.

"No, I didn't feel any drops," said Derek. "Why?"

"It's getting so dark."

"All those clouds, I expect. I hope to goodness it doesn't." And Derek peered up at the sky. "Looks pretty gloomy," he admitted. "Perhaps we'd better stay here for a bit, and keep dry. It'll probably pass over."

They settled themselves again and lay for a while, quietly reflecting.

"Well built hut, this," said Derek at length. "We ought to try and make a place like it, if we camp in the forest with Crusoe. He could help us chop the poles—he's got an axe. You drive in a double row and then fill the space between them with bracken. How are they fixed?" He got up again and began to examine the joints. "Simple as anything; just nails and a wire splicing. And branches for the roof. Must be fairly weatherproof, it's all dry as a bone inside."

"Think of the bracken you'd need," said Diana. "It's squeezed down tight as tight."

Derek waved a hand towards the forest. "Easily cut as much as you need," he said airily.

"Derek, are you sure it isn't raining?"

"Positive. We'd hear the noise if it was."

"But it's getting pitchy dark."

"Hardly that," said Derek. "Might be a thunderstorm brewing, of course. Remember how dark it went, that time with the circus?"

Diana remembered.

"Still thirsty?" Derek asked her a few minutes later. "Like a bit of chocolate now?"

"Hadn't we better keep it? We haven't anything else to eat."

"Perhaps we ought to," said Derek, disappointed. "We'll make a start, walking again, as soon as this storm's passed over. I think . . ."

"Yes?" Diana prompted, for Derek was hesitating.

"I think we'd better go back to Dalehurst," Derek continued. "And sleep the night there, like you said yesterday. By the time we get to the Forest Road . . ."

"We mustn't get caught in the dark," said Diana.

"Just what I was thinking," nodded Derek. "If only this storm would blow over. I can't see that it's getting lighter, yet."

"It *is* a black sky," said Diana, moving across to the entrance of the hut and staring up beyond the tops of the trees. "It's going to simply *pour* in a minute."

They both looked out into the gloomy depths of the forest. A short while ago, so it seemed, all had been painted in shades of a light grey; trees, sky, and the distant haze between the trunks. Now, with the dark clouds shutting them in, the trees stood like grim sentinels; their black, shadowy branches reaching up and almost merging with the sky. Inside the hut all was shadowy, too. There was scarcely enough light, now, for them to see into the far corners. And still the relentless clouds thickened and still the light dimmed; seeping away as gradually as water leaves a basin when the waste-pipe is blocked; leaving the dark things first; lingering on the paler surfaces of their hands and faces, and on an old torn corner of newspaper lying just outside the hut.

As they watched, they listened, intently, for the first few splashes of rain to strike the crisp bracken; followed soon by the steady, whispering murmur of the storm, gathering strength and volume as it swept over the forest. But nothing disturbed the silence save a few, faint chirps of sleepy birds; deceived, perhaps, by the sudden darkness into thinking that this was the dusk; the nightfall. And then Derek, staring out from the shelter, realized that he could no longer distinguish the shapes even of the nearest trees; all was merging into a uniform, blurred and shadowy mass; colourless and darker, but not much darker, than the sky.

He looked at his sister and she looked back at him. They were both frightened; oppressed by the weight of this black gloom. No storm they had ever experienced had made things as dark as this. What could be going to happen? Was this silence the stillness of expectation; the hush before the storm broke over their heads? Even the birds had stopped chirping. And still the silence remained unbroken and still the darkness grew thicker and closed in around them.

Derek found that Diana was crouching against him, holding his arm. They had retreated farther inside the hut and were waiting, shoulders hunched, almost as if they expected the sky to fall. For a few moments he thought wildly of an eclipse. Then a faint suspicion dawned in his mind; he wavered, and like a shaft of light, he suddenly understood. A black weight seemed to lift off his mind and in his relief he forgot all about their situation; sheltering in a bracken hut, miles from anywhere; lost in the heart of the forest.

"Di, it's all right!" he cried. "We've made a mistake. We must have walked for much longer than we thought. There isn't going to be any storm." He laughed, and as his sister looked at him, not understanding, Derek stretched an arm, pointing into the darkness outside. "It won't get light again," he explained. "Not till to-morrow. It's beginning to be night-time, that's all. And to think we've been feeling scared of that!"

CHAPTER 10

Bracken for Bedding

NIGHT-TIME! So night was falling already? They had been walking all the late afternoon and evening, following Derek's endless circle through the forest, and now, very little farther on, and completely lost, they were marooned in the darkness inside this bracken hut, and here they would have to stay for hours and hours, right through the night, with no blankets to warm them and nothing to eat. Diana felt no weight lifted from her mind. On the contrary, she would have preferred a storm, any storm, no matter how violent, to this.

"But, Derek," she managed to gasp. "We'll have to spend the night—we'll have to *sleep* here!" She sounded utterly horrified at the prospect.

Derek's practical mind was already a jump ahead. He saw, too, that his sister was working herself up and that the sooner she was occupied the better. If they hadn't been able to find their way through the forest by daylight, they would, of course, stand no chance at all in the dark. They must stay here and thank their lucky stars that they had found such an adequate shelter. He said so, aloud, and before Diana could protest any further he shoved Titch's penknife into her hand and demanded dry bracken, plenty of it.

"We'll use it as bedding," he said. "There isn't enough here to cover us properly and lie on. I'll start collecting firewood. Lucky I brought those matches."

"You'll set the whole hut alight . . ."

"Outside, of course, in front here. I'll clear a space,

don't you worry. Come on, we must make the most of it, before it gets really dark. I don't want to use the torch too much."

They groped their way through the thick dusk and soon the quiet of the forest was broken by the crack and splinter of dead branches and the rustle of bracken as Diana hacked away at the tough stalks with the penknife Derek had found. Collecting firewood went much more easily, and in a short while quite a substantial heap lay by the entrance of the hut.

"Beastly scratchy job," Diana complained, as Derek went to help her. "You can't see the brambles. I haven't gathered very much yet, I'm afraid."

They worked on, stooping, cutting, tugging and then piling the crisp fronds together, until they could hardly make out their hands in front of them. Derek went for his torch and they carried light, unsubstantial bundles of bedding into the hut. They filled one corner and piled it almost to the roof before Derek was satisfied.

"Now," he said, "I'll light a fire and then we'll put on all the clothes we've got. I don't think we shall be cold. We shall just be hungry."

"Good thing Brian isn't here," said Diana, beginning to smile again, and Derek, remembering their friend's appetite, chuckled as he selected the driest of his twigs and built a little wigwam in the space he had cleared for the fire.

He used as kindling the scrap of newspaper and some bracken from the floor of the hut. The tiny fire smouldered and went out at Derek's first attempt. He persevered, and the third match set it going in fine style. He fed it with larger sticks and soon the flames caught hold in real earnest and flickered up like a camp fire really should.

The inside of the hut was bathed in a cheerful rosy light. Everything outside went a shade or two blacker and became completely invisible. As he sat back on his heels, contented with his handiwork, Derek caught his sister's glowing eyes as she bent forward, face towards the fire.

"Derek," she breathed, with the air of one who makes a tremendous and surprising discovery. "I think—I really think this is going to be *fun!*"

"It might be if we had some eats," said Derek. "That's going to be the trouble. We shall be starving by to-morrow morning. I feel famished already."

They unpacked the rucksacks by the light of the fire, and spread their contents on the bracken floor. Derek stripped to his shirt and put on a second one. He then put on two pullovers, one over the other; the long-sleeved, blue one on top. His coat felt absurdly tight and constricted under the armpits when he struggled into it again, and the buttons would scarcely do up. Finally he put on his mackintosh and felt ready for anything; even a night at sea.

Diana was doing the same and the two stuffed dumplings regarded each other in the warm, dancing light. "Stockings," said Derek. "A dry pair, and bedroom slippers. *We* shall be all right."

They could hardly bend to sit down, and once down, felt they could never possibly get up again.

"I'm stifling," said Diana. "The fire's getting hot, now. Don't let's wear *every*thing yet, it's silly. We may be cold later on to-night."

Derek allowed the sense of this, and they shed their outer garments. A further search of the almost empty rucksacks revealed a paper bag of sandwiches which, somehow, had been overlooked and had made it's way down to the bottom of Derek's pack. This was treasure trove indeed, and was handled lovingly and a minute count made of the contents. Part was portioned off for "breakfast"; the others they consumed there and then; chewing every mouthful for at least a minute and spinning the meal out for as long as they could. A square of chocolate, two for Diana, completed supper, after which they both became more than ever conscious of an aching thirst.

"We *must* find something to drink," said Derek. "Is there a stream near? Did we pass one, d'you remember?"

"Yes, we crossed a bridge. I'm sure I remember," cried Diana, quite excited. "There was a log in the water, and it was all overgrown. I said we'd never been there before."

"Could you find it if we went with the torch?"

"I might," Diana hesitated. "But we mustn't go together. Just think, if we couldn't find the hut again."

"There's the fire!" Derek stretched out for some more wood to feed the flames. "We should see the light."

Diana was not convinced. "You stay here and we'll keep calling to each other," she said. "As long as I could hear you, I don't think I'd mind."

"But we've nothing to bring back the water in!"

"I'll have a drink first, and then you can go and I'll stay and call."

Derek handed her the torch and stood outside the hut; his stockinged feet brightly lit. All around was a circle of inky blackness; a wall of dark beyond the farthest reach of the flames. And Diana was going to walk out into that pitchy dark and the night and the trees would swallow her up.

"Won't be long," she said, gulping a little, and as she pressed the button on the shiny silver side of the torch, the beam of light wavered, for her hand was not quite steady. "You'll keep on shouting, won't you?"

Derek watched her go; her faintly lit back melting into the shadows like a ghost. Then only the tiny pool of light from the torch was visible, moving jerkily along, and Derek called out, feeling a little self-conscious to be shouting for no apparent reason—and the forest was very, very quiet. Diana's high voice answered him and he stood there, his legs warm, almost too hot; shouting at intervals and hearing her replies grow gradually softer as she moved farther and farther away.

Diana, out in the blackness, felt the trees as presences which she could not see. They were standing all around her, trunks and branches leaning inwards, straining, straining down, and through the tunnel they made she hurried, groping along, with only the spot of light flung by the torch on the ground for company. The darkness was solid; so solid that she often put up an arm, instinctively, to protect her face. Now and then she heard Derek hail her, and turning to shout back, saw the pinpoint of their fire twinkling like a star come down to earth, far, far away behind.

She was following one of the paths; the torch painted a brilliant emerald circle of grass in front of her feet. She hoped she was going the right way, and kept a sharp ear open for the rippling sound of the stream, but she could not be too sure. The clearing had seemed quite different, in the dark, and she had chosen her direction almost blindly. But something told her she was all right; that she would find the stream a little farther along the track, and Diana was not surprised to hear the noise of running water and to find, quite suddenly, that she had reached the bridge.

E

The stream glinted and sparkled as she pointed the light down, and the same, waterlogged trunk of a tree, black and glistening, interrupted the even flow. Before she knelt to drink Diana turned and switched off the torch, the better to peer through the blackness, but nowhere could she see any sign of the camp fire.

"Derek!" she called, as loud as she could. "I've found the stream!" and as his voice replied, incredibly faint and distant, she repeated the single word "water" three times. The forest might have been a desert; the stream an oasis! And pressing the button of the torch, she scrambled down the bank almost underneath the bridge, and kneeling, her hair falling forward, the tips draggling and wet, she sucked noisily; gulping mouthfuls of the cold, beautiful liquid.

Something scrabbled and splashed in the shadows under the brick arch and she started and nearly let the torch fall into the stream. A rat? Her knees would be muddy after this; she could feel the soft, sticky press of the bank as she knelt, drinking. Was the water clean? Somehow, in the dark, this didn't seem to matter greatly, and from what she could see, it looked pure enough and tasted—well, it tasted at least a hundred times nicer than the water served in a glass jug on the dining-room table at home.

Refreshed and much happier, she guided herself back through the forest, first by the invisible rope of Derek's voice, hauling her in as steadily as a fisherman lands his catch; and then by the sparkling pinprick twinkle of their fire, visible again through the trees. Derek had changed into his walking shoes and was ready and impatiently waiting his turn for a drink.

"It's lovely," said Diana, handing him the torch.

"And quite easy to get to. I'll come across the clearing with you and show you the path."

After another five minutes of shouting Derek returned, as refreshed as his sister. They stoked the fire and began to arrange the bracken bedding and settle themselves to sleep.

"If we put a good thick layer underneath, as a mattress," said Derek, "and then some more over us and our macks on top of it all, to hold it down, we should keep jolly warm."

"Can't we stuff the rucksacks and use them as pillows?" suggested Diana.

Derek thought this was an excellent scheme. They worked busily for a few minutes and then Diana stretched herself out for a trial. Derek heaped a mountain of bracken on top of her and, draping the mackintosh across, pressed it down into shape.

"Pouf!" said Diana, wrinkling her nose. "Stop, it's prickly. You're scratching my face to bits. I think I'm going to—to sneeze." And she did.

"Dust," said Derek. "We're lucky it's so dry. The sun to-day must have helped a lot."

"It's my feet that are the trouble," Diana complained, lifting her head as high as she could and trying to see over the pile of bracken. "They're sticking out."

"The mackintosh isn't long enough," said Derek. "Either your shoulders or your feet are bound to stick out, I'm afraid."

Diana resigned herself to the inevitable.

"Comfortable?" inquired Derek, surveying her.

"Yes, fairly," Diana admitted, in a cautious voice. "Ground's a bit hard."

"You've got plenty of bracken under you," said Derek.

"It's prickly," said Diana. "Beastly round my neck."

Derek grunted in a grown-up, ought-to-be-thankful-for-what-you've-got sort of way, and sat down beside his sister. He heaped the rest of the bracken on top of himself, flung his mack over it, and lay back on the rucksack pillow. He hastily raised his head, however, and turned the pillow buckle side down. This done, he grunted again in a more satisfied way, and settled himself into a comfortable position for the night.

"Warm?" he inquired of Diana.

"Warm as toast, thanks. It's getting colder, though, isn't it?"

Derek agreed that it was. "We shall be all right as long as the fire keeps going. But those sticks burn so quickly."

"I wish we had a big rug we could spread over us, feet and all," said Diana wistfully.

"Think of having to carry it to-morrow. *I* don't," said Derek. "I'd like some food though. I'd like something hot. I'd like . . ."

"Think of us yesterday," said Diana. "Supper all to ourselves. Lovely asparagus."

"We *have* done some queer things," said Derek. "Sleeping one night in a strange house and the next in the forest. Di, d'you feel at all afraid, being out here?"

Diana hesitated. "Funny you should ask that," she said. "I was just thinking. I suppose I ought to, really. I don't *like* it, of course, but that's not the same as feeling properly scared."

"No lions and tigers and things, anyway," said Derek. "Not much to be afraid of in England. If we were camping out we shouldn't worry one bit."

"Good thing Mummy doesn't know what we're doing."

"*She'd* worry," said Derek. "But I don't believe Daddy

would. We'll be able to tell them, afterwards, when everything's come out right."

"After all, it isn't anyone's fault . . ."

"Oh, it's mine," Derek admitted. "But I didn't *want* to go walking round in circles. Who would?"

"Derek," said Diana, changing the subject, "d'you feel sorry for Cynthia? I do, terribly."

"Must be awful, of course, not being able to move your legs. But I suppose if you've never done it, you don't miss it so much."

"Oh, but, Derek, she does! You can see she feels it dreadfully. That's why I think we should help her."

There was a pause. Derek made no remark.

"Just because we're lucky," Diana continued, "we oughtn't to forget all about her. We can go off. She's stuck there all the time. Mrs. Potts is jolly nice, I know, but . . ."

"A day with Mrs. Potts would send me potty!" Derek agreed.

"That's what I mean. We ought to help her get away and do things with us."

"But we don't really know them," Derek protested, roused at last. "How can we? We were never meant to stay at all, and we can't very well go back again. Besides, she's got her cousins there, now. And we've never even met her mother. We only spent the night there because of that old lady's mad idea. . . ."

"She rescued us!" cried Diana, roused in her turn. "You were ready enough for her to help *us*. Now you want to stop me helping Cynthia."

"No, I don't—I mean . . ."

"You do. You don't like her just because she's clever and teases you."

"Shut up!" roared Derek, quite angry by this time. "I'm not going to argue. Cynthia's all right. But we can't take her away from her family. We're strangers, don't you understand?"

Diana subsided; still a little resentful. She looked up at the sloping roof of boughs, laid evenly side by side; lit by the fire through the open end of the shelter. The thick, snug walls of bracken enclosed them; the scent of the dead, dry fronds was everywhere and bracken tickled her under the chin. When she stirred, it whispered and crackled. The fire was burning low; a heap of red ashes crowned with a few short flickering tongues of flame. Derek had put on the last of the wood; from now on the hut would get colder and colder. She glanced sideways at her brother; lying on his back, his jaw still stuck out obstinately. She could see his profile dark against the glow from the fire. He was most probably right; he usually was. Stupid of them to have so nearly quarrelled.

"Derek," she whispered in a softer voice. "Are you asleep?"

"Nearly."

"Mind if I talk?"

"Well, don't harp, will you?"

"No, not about Cynthia. Derek, d'you remember those knockers?"

"The owl and the peacock?"

"Yes. Did you like them?"

"Quite."

"Be nice to have them at home."

"Those ones?"

"One's like them. D'you remember what Mrs. Potts said?"

"No," said Derek yawning.

"Don't you? About beauty and wisdom?"

"Oh, *that!*"

"Well, you were second in your class . . ."

"Third," said Derek, a stickler for accuracy. "And I suppose you think you're beautiful."

"Don't be a pig," said Diana in a pleased voice.

Derek turned, rustling the bracken coverlet, and tried to see her face. He had never thought of his sister in terms of someone who, one day, would or would not be good looking. But by the tone of her voice he judged that the question had begun to interest her.

"You probably will be, when you're older," he said encouragingly. "You're not bad now, really. A bit spotty."

"Pig," cried Diana, in quite a different voice. She turned away from him, greatly incensed.

"You'll grow out of them," said Derek. "But why d'you want to be beautiful? I thought you said once, you'd never go and get married."

"So I did," said Diana startled, turning back again. "I won't. Why . . . ?"

"Lot of fuss I call it," said Derek. "Worrying about what you look like."

"I want people to turn round and stare at me when I come into a room," said Diana. "And I shouldn't mind. I should know I was the most beautiful person there."

Derek guffawed. A piece of bracken got into his mouth and he choked and tried to claw it out with his fingers.

"Go to sleep," he advised. "You'll feel better in the morning. Punch me if I start to snore." And with a great heaving and rustling he settled himself again, head on his rucksack.

The fire glowed; a puddle of red ash on the ground outside. The forest trees stood very still; scarcely a branch or a twig stirred in all the miles of woodland. The darkness hung like a thick curtain round the hut and soon, in spite of the hard floor and prickly bracken, a quiet, steady rhythm of breathing showed that the only two people in the forest were already sound asleep.

CHAPTER 11

Babes in the Wood

"Slep' the night in the forest, 'ave you?" The driver of the milk lorry banged the palm of his hand against the steering wheel. "All by your little selves, bless us, and what will Mum and Dad be thinking about it, eh?" His voice bellowed lustily over the combined roar of the engine and the jangle and vibration of the double row of tall churns loaded in the back. "Minute I caught sight o' the two of you 'long there on the road, I says to myself, what's this? I says. Six in the morning and not a bloomin' 'ouse for miles and miles; nothing but trees!" The huge, red-faced, cheery man waved his right hand out of the window, pointing to the endless border of forest. "*Trees!*" he repeated, with biting contempt. "No good to no-one, they aren't! Oughter be cut down and made into chairs and tables and cupboards for the use of folks like us! Build some nice little 'ouses out there, you could—build 'em in rows, close together. Cosy-like."

Derek struggled weakly against the torrent of noise. He felt dazed and bleary-eyed; quite unable to face up to the persistent, shattering foghorn of a voice roaring at him above the tumult. How gladly would he have crawled down and away from the world into the silence and blackness of some safe hole. He felt completely exhausted; every jolt and jar of the lorry pushed him about, and all the time he was fighting with his eyes—they *would* keep shutting—and stifling down enormous, devastating yawns that seemed to rise up inside him and threaten to burst his throat. He was troubled, too, with a strange, queasy feeling; he didn't know whether he was beginning to feel sick, or whether he was just terribly hungry; hungry far beyond the usual grumbling ache.

Diana, hunched close beside him and leaning her head back against the cab door, had closed her eyes. Her mouth was half-open and her face had absolutely no colour; her cheeks might have been made of putty. Derek wondered if the bumping, swaying movement of the lorry and the fumes of the engine were making her feel as funny as he did. What was the man saying? Something about houses in the forest? How much farther to go, before they reached a town and could find some breakfast? They were lucky to have got a lift like this; he oughtn't to complain. But it was all such a racket and the driver *would* keep talking and expecting him to answer. Now that he knew they'd slept the night out, he would give them no peace at all.

"We're not staying anywhere yet," he said wearily in reply to further loud-voiced questions. "We've been trying to find our friend—he's got a horse and caravan —but he wasn't where we thought he was and we got lost coming back."

"Lost in all them trees?"

"We went in circles," said Derek, and then explained about the bracken hut. "We slept quite well at first, until we woke up and it was still the middle of the night and the fire had gone out and we couldn't keep warm. We tried and tried, but we didn't go to sleep again. The ground was jolly hard, too. We waited for hours until it began to grow light and then we started walking again and this time we did reach the road."

" 'Aven't you 'ad any breakfast?"

"A sandwich each and a bit of chocolate."

"What d'you say to a nice 'ot cup o' tea and a rasher or two of bacon with a fried egg on toast," shouted the lorry driver with an encouraging grin. "Bless me, you must be fair perished! I was stopping at Freddie's myself, feelin' the need o' something 'ot and wet, as most of us do these sharp mornings! Hold tight to yourselves and I'll push her on a bit."

And with the engine steadily blaring and all the milk churns jolting and rattling to the rhythm of the wheels, they rocketed down the Forest Road.

"We came along here before," Derek thought to himself. "The day before yesterday, in another lorry—going the other way!" Quite soon, the trees gave place to green fields where mist still lingered, and cows and horses added their white breath to the haze. The forest was some miles behind them before the lorry driver slowed his pace, and with his arm signalled a sharp right turn across the road. Through the windscreen Derek glimpsed a tiny wooden shanty, painted bright green; a little house dwarfed by the giant shapes of lorries parked on the strip of ground outside.

" 'Ere we are again," said their new friend cheerily. "And a lot of the boys before us. You ain't 'ad your whack of shut-eye, 'ave you mate!" This last to Diana, who was struggling to rouse herself. "Come along now and trust your uncle." He lifted her down from the cab and marched them between the lorries, across to the door of the little shack. Painted in dirty white letters along one of the boards they read the single word *Freddies*. The door had glass panes, all steamy and moist, and, as they entered, a wall of hot air met them; the atmosphere inside was thick with the mingled smells of cooking and cigarette smoke. Derek swallowed and felt violently sick. The cool breath of the early morning had revived him; he had felt better just walking across from the lorry, but *this* . . . They stumbled forward behind the vast bulk of the lorry driver, and heard the steady growl of deep voices falter and pause and then break out again louder than before, as the men sitting at the small square tables shouted and exchanged jokes and stared curiously at the newcomers.

" 'Ullo, Pete, brought the kids along with you? Where's the missus? Trust you to leave *'er* at home. Wot's all this 'ere? Blinkin' school treat I calls it. Proper family man, ain't he?"

Diana, raising her eyes nervously, thought she had never seen such a collection of tough, dirty looking men before. The room was crowded with them; every table seemed occupied, and as all heads were turned in their direction, greyish, stubbly faces swam through the drifting smoke. Thick white mugs of strong tea; white plates; hunks of bread littered the tables, and somewhere over at the far end of the room she made out a counter piled high with crocks. Behind this counter; almost hidden from view by a tall urn with a spirit lamp underneath, stood a little thin-faced man in a stained white coat.

"Mornin', Freddie!" bawled the driver of the milk lorry, making his way across the room with Derek and Diana in tow. "Noisy lot o' fellers you've got 'ere, 'aven't you. When are you going to teach 'em manners? Three cups o' tea, 'ot and sweet, and pile up a plate o' fry each for the kiddies. Everything you've got. They ain't had what you could call a bite for longer than's good for 'em."

The thin-faced man obediently rattled mugs and

spoons together; turned on the tap of the urn, filled a dirty teapot and sloshed out the muddy liquid. Then he vanished into what appeared to be a small kitchen; there was a great sound of sizzling and spluttering before the door closed behind him. Meanwhile, their friend had turned to face the room; his thumbs stuck in his waistcoat pockets; a knowing grin all over his round, ruddy face.

"Slep' the night in the forest, they 'ave," he announced, as soon as he could make himself heard. "Not campin' out, mind you. They lost their way. Can you beat it?" And he nodded his head towards Derek and Diana. "Bless me if there ain't a bit o' bracken left in 'er 'air now!" And to Diana's embarrassment he disentangled a small fragment of last night's bedding and held it up for inspection. There was an immediate roar of laughter; chairs were pushed back and "Proper babes in the wood! Did you ever know the like!" bellowed a huge man in dungarees, pushing his way towards them.

"Now then, clear a table," said their friend, placing himself in front of them. He was well satisfied with the sensation he had created. "They don't want no questions now. They wants a bite to eat, don't you, mates?"

Derek nodded faintly, wondering how on earth he would ever manage to swallow anything. He was literally swaying on his feet. They flopped on to the chairs provided for them and willing hands pushed mugs of tea under their noses.

"You down that, youngster," somebody said. "You'll feel better. Looks as sorry for himself as a sick cat."

"Thanks," Derek managed to gasp, and gulped a mouthful of the hot, brown liquid. It left a film on the roof of his mouth, but he began to feel the better for it.

He looked across to see how Diana was doing. The large man in the dark-blue dungarees was bending over her, watching her drink. He raised his head at that moment and winked at one of the other drivers. "Proper little toffs," he grinned.

Derek felt inclined to resent this remark, but a plate was clapped in front of him, piled with food, and a knife and fork to eat it with, and he had to summon up all his resources. The smell of fried bacon made him feel faint again. He toyed with a small piece, but such half-hearted measures did not satisfy the crowd. They might have been at the zoo, these men, watching the lions being fed! "Look at 'im! Wants a glass o' milk and a biscuit!" came a taunting voice. This settled Derek. He took a really good mouthful and somehow managed to swallow it. The next went down more easily. He almost enjoyed the third. Was he hungry? Was he *famished!* And across the square table Diana, too, was tucking in for all she was worth; the colour slowly creeping back into her cheeks again.

Pete, the driver of the milk lorry, stood over them while they were eating with a great air of proprietorship, for he was a showman born. These kiddies were good entertainment, and Pete had a reputation to keep up. He was well known at this "pull-in" café for drivers, where the long-distance men with their huge, multi-wheeled lorries and trailers, stopped off for breakfast after an all-night run from the North. Even Freddie himself was standing, hands on the counter, watching the new arrivals over the heaped plates.

"Picked 'em up about four miles out o' Dalehurst," Pete was saying, between swigs of tea. "Lonely spot, that. Not an 'ouse nowhere, nothing but trees. Six o'clock in the morning. Slep' in an 'ut, they did. Bracken 'ut. No more to cover 'em than what they've got on."

"Except some loose bracken," Derek added. "Too cold for me. I wouldn't want to do it again."

"On the look out for a friend, they are. Travelling with an 'orse and caravan." (A renewed growl of astonishment from the circle of men, grouped close about them.) "If any of you blokes 'appens to 'ave passed him on the road . . ."

"If I remember rightly, I saw one of them caravans back in Dalehurst," said a driver, a yellow stub of cigarette waggling as he spoke. "Parked off the road, it was."

"No, he's travelling with the gypsies," Derek, after a moment's hesitation, shook his head. "That couldn't be him. He's going down to the sea with them, we know. We want to catch him up."

"Who's heading for the coast?" asked Pete. "I can't give 'em a lift much farther, myself."

"I'll take 'em along," volunteered the man in dungarees. "I'm going down to Littleport. You can smell the sea from there," he added for Derek and Diana's benefit. "Even if you can't see it. On an estuary."

"D'you think the gypsies will have gone that way?" Derek asked a little doubtfully.

" 'Ere, George, you've come up from the coast this morning. See any gyppos?"

The man called George shook his head. "Dark most o' the way," he explained. "Tell you what, though! I saw somewheres they was building up a fair—roundabouts and coconut shies, you know the sort o' thing!"

"Did you, my lad!" said Pete excitedly. "And I'll tell *you* that a fair'll draw every gyppo in the county as sure as eggs is eggs. Attracts 'em like wasps to a honey pot, ain't that so?"

No-one contradicted him and they all waited for the man called George to tell them the name of the town or village.

"Did you come up through Littleport? What time was it, lad? Was it dark?"

"Yes," George nodded his head. He had seen their lamps. "They were building up early-like," he said.

Pete, quick as a knife, rattled out a list of names, but George only looked more than ever confused. All that anyone could gather was that somewhere along the coast road past Littleport he had seen a fair in process of erection. Further details he could not give.

"That's your bird, mates," said Pete, turning triumphantly to Derek and Diana. "Your pal will be there, as sure as a duck'll swim. Ernie here will take you to Littleport and put you on the right road. Nother cup o' tea for you? And for your little sister? Three more splashes from the pot, chum!" And he banged their thick mugs on the counter.

Derek put down his knife and fork, bewildered. The speed with which their future movements were being arranged for them was baffling! He hoped that it was all right. Difficult to say anything, really; these lorry drivers were so friendly and well meaning and were quite convinced they had solved the problem. Diana was looking rather worried, but they couldn't do anything better than this, could they? He was beginning to feel sleepier than ever, now that he had polished off the plate of hot fry. The second mug of tea and a thick doorstep off the loaf, spread with marmalade, completed breakfast, and he was quite relieved when, at last, the

men around him began to make a move. Several pushed
through the door; shouting greetings and wishing them
all the best of luck. Then, together with their friend
Pete and the man in dungarees, they left the little shack;
shivering in the cool air outside. The noise was tremendous
as lorry after lorry started up, backed, turned and crawled
out on the road again; they seemed to pulse with the
thunder of the engines.

"Up you get," said their new driver, and he opened
the door of the biggest lorry of them all. The cab itself,
Derek saw, was detached from the main, tarpaulin-
covered body; and then again there was a division where
a trailer was coupled on; each section jointed so that the
whole could turn more easily. This gave more the effect
of a train than of a lorry; indeed, it was quite the largest
thing on four—on *fourteen*—wheels that Derek had ever
seen. Why, the great, heavily-treaded tyres came up
almost to his chin! And up in the cab, they might have
been standing in the covered bridge of an ocean liner!

Before they moved off, they had to lean down and
grasp Pete the lorry driver's hand. Solemnly, he said
good-bye to them and repeated his assurances. "You'll
find your pal," he said. "Mark my words. You'll find him
at that there fairground as sure as . . ." But his last
words were drowned in the deep roar of the engine as
the man in dungarees started her up, and Pete had to
step aside and slam the door as the huge lorry nosed
cautiously out on to the road.

CHAPTER 12

Troublesome Trio

MICHAEL and Titch were up in the morning early; splashing in the bucket that hung underneath the waggon before Crusoe himself showed any signs of stirring. They had pitched their tent next door to the caravan and, as Titch had remarked yesterday evening, crawling into his sleeping-bag, it was all quite like old times again!

"Derek and Diana are coming to-day," said Michael, scrubbing his teeth and spitting vigorously. "I wonder what bus they'll catch. We could go and meet them."

"Oh they'll turn up," said Titch. "Crusoe said he'd sent them a wire, so they'll know where to find us."

"Titch, are you hungry?"

"Hollow," said Michael's large brother, slapping himself.

"Can you eat a biscuit or something? Don't let's wake up Crusoe yet, let's go and see that nest again, before breakfast."

"The long-tailed tit's?"

Michael nodded, swinging his sponge-bag.

"All right," said Titch. "I'll try for some grub. The tin's in the caravan." And, very carefully, he began to climb the steps leading up to the door. "Don't think I'll disturb him," he whispered. "He said he was going to do some work last night."

"Midnight oil," breathed Michael to himself. (What fun, to be able to stay up for as long as you liked, just whenever you pleased!) There was a small scrape, as of a tin on the waggon floor, and then Titch reappeared, climbing down backwards and hugging the biscuits to his chest.

"He always has this kind," said Michael, helping himself. Chocolate digestives—just the thing for an early-morning snack!

They stuffed two each into the pockets of their shorts and, leaving the tin inside the tent, they walked across the grass to the forest's edge; the trail of their footprints straggling dark through the light dew. Their gym shoes were soaked almost immediately and they felt the chill wetness on their feet. A faint mist still hung about, low on the ground, and the trees seemed to be floating, light and airy; no longer anchored by their roots. Everywhere they breathed the same damp fresh smell.

"We ought to be able to find more different *kinds* of nests," Michael was complaining. "Instead of only thrushes and blackbirds."

"Give us a chance," said Titch. "We haven't really looked yet. They build big nests, low down; you can't miss 'em, with the hedges still bare. Most birds wait till the leaves come out."

"We were lucky finding this one . . ." Michael lowered his voice as they turned off the path into a dense thicket. They had to worm their way through between high domes of bramble; dense and impenetrable masses of dry, thorny shoots. Michael paused in front of one of these bushes and peered inside; shuffling sideways and ducking his head clear of the trailing strands.

"Bit farther along," whispered Titch, giving him a nudge. "There you are." And they both gazed at the little round, lichen-green ball of grass and moss hung safely inside the interlacing brambles.

"You could have cupped the nest in the hollow of your hands," Michael said afterwards, telling Crusoe all about it at breakfast. "And there was a little hole, like a mouse hole, in the side—you'd never think a bird could have got in that way. We were standing watching when we saw a head was poking out; you could see the beak and eyes. And then out it fluttered, tiny body and great long tail, and went dodging through the bush—the brambles were so thick you couldn't put your hand in, but it found a way and wriggled through like smoke and flew away with its tail streaming after it!"

"We stood farther off and waited," said Titch, taking up the tale, "and sure enough, back it came again. It only half went into the nest—we saw the tail sticking out of the hole for quite a long time."

"Probably feeding her babies," put in Michael. "Crusoe, would the eggs have hatched out as early as this?"

"It is on the early side," Crusoe seemed to think. "But I expect she's got a family. You found a blackbird with young yesterday, didn't you?"

Michael nodded. "Crusoe, will you come and help us find more different *kinds* of nests?"

"Not started out as an egg collector, have you?"

"Well, I did think of that," said Michael candidly. "But then I got a better idea. I collect the whole thing— nest and eggs and birds and everything."

Crusoe looked startled. The coffeepot held at an angle over his cup, he stared across the table. "You *what?*" he said.

"I'll show you," Michael exclaimed eagerly. "I left it in here—or did I have it in the tent? I've got one of those exercise books," he continued, staring round the waggon.

"The sort you can write in and draw in. Won't be a minute!" And he wriggled out of his seat on one of the bunks and dived through the open door and down the steps.

Titch leant back and stretched himself. "Latest craze!" he said with a grin. "Nature log book."

Crusoe looked greatly relieved and poured out his coffee. "So that's it! I thought his collecting sounded a bit whole-hogged."

"I did some bird's nesting once, at school," said Titch ruminatively. "Got stuck up on top of a tree and *I* couldn't get down. Had to fetch ropes and ladders and goodness knows what. I was ragged about it, I can tell you. They said I was more trouble than the headmaster's cat. She was always getting stuck up in trees."

"Bird's nesting, too?" asked Crusoe.

"Chased by dogs, I think," said Titch.

Michael reappeared; clattering up the steps with a bright green exercise book in his hand. Crusoe pushed away plates and cups and saucers and made room for him.

"This is my idea," puffed Michael. "Couldn't find it for ages. It was in my sleeping-bag." He bent back a corner that was creased. On the green cover, a little indistinct because the ink had dried a light shade, Crusoe read the title of the work. *Nature Log Book. Michael Crosbie*.

"I did all this at home, before I came," said the author, turning over a title-page executed in three different coloured inks and an almost blank page headed *Contents*. Only three items were listed there, so far.

"You see, I don't enter any kind twice. That's why I want to find other sorts of nests." Michael turned to page one. The ruled, left-hand page, was headed THRUSH, and below he had written a description of the first thrush's nest he had found, telling exactly where it was built and the number of eggs it had contained—followed by a description of the parent birds and their reactions when the nest was discovered. On the opposite page, a white sheet of drawing paper, he had illustrated his text with a painting of the nest and it's cluster of blue, speckly eggs, wedged in the crook of a holly-tree, and below this, with a fine drawing of a parent thrush.

"I copied that from my bird book," said Michael. "I had to, really, to get the details right. If I get better at it, I'll try and draw from memory."

Crusoe nodded; brought out his pipe and tobacco-pouch from his pocket and began to fill the bowl. Michael, glancing at him anxiously for an opinion, noticed the reddy-gold roughness of his chin; Crusoe shaved after the breakfast wash-up, when there was boiling water in the kettle. He was reading every word about the thrushes. Michael felt a glow; a warmth of fellow-feeling. Here was somebody who was really interested; who wanted to see what he had done. Titch was better than no-one, but being an elder brother, exercised his right to tease. Besides, Titch was never quite serious. You could count on Crusoe. Michael noticed, once again, what a curious sharp, strong face was his; Crusoe always reminded him of the portraits of Indian braves in his illustrated edition of *Hiawatha*. Put a feather head-dress on his untidy mop of fair hair; place a tomahawk in his hand; stain his fresh, red face a deeper brown, and he would have been a Red Indian chieftain to the life!

"Yes," said Crusoe, interrupting his train of thought. "You've certainly got something here. Just a moment while I light my pipe."

The match sputtered; he pulled vigorously, puffing out clouds of smoke which drifted up around the tarnished brass of the lamp, hung from a hook in the ceiling.

"Let's have a look at the blackbird," he said, and Michael turned the page. There was the painting of the nest, on the left this time, and instead of a group of eggs Michael had drawn the gaping red throats of five hungry youngsters, beaks open, heads upturned.

"Hot stuff!" Crusoe murmured. "You've got the idea, all right. You're improving, you know. These are better than the drawings you did last summer."

"I haven't finished the long-tailed tit," said Michael. "I've only drawn in the first rough sketch. I'd like to paint the bird wriggling through all those brambles."

"You've got a difficult subject there," Crusoe puffed away at his pipe, reading what Michael had written about the blackbird. "But the idea's first-class. I don't see why you should only collect birds and their nests. You call your book 'Nature Log.' What about wild animals, and flowers and . . ."

"You don't see so very many animals," said Michael. "Except rabbits, perhaps, and they're not so nice to draw. And they're *so* many different kinds of flowers. I just feel like collecting birds' nests."

"What about butterflies, then?" Crusoe suggested. "Plenty of colour there."

Michael thought this an excellent idea. "I could start them at the other end," he said. "I've seen some bright yellow ones in the forest . . ."

"Brimstones," said Crusoe. "As a matter of fact, I

could help you more with butterflies and moths than I could with birds. I know quite a bit about them. I used to collect them when I was younger, but I stopped after a while. It was so difficult not to damage them, and then they seemed to lose so much of their beauty, stuck in rows in a glass case. You can't preserve them as they actually are—almost as bad as pressing flowers. But you could paint them feeding and flying. This is one of the best places in England, you know; you get a lot of different kinds here, but of course it's too early in the year for most of them. Those Brimstones are always among the first out; they hibernate through the winter and the warm sun in March and April wakes 'em up."

"I've seen another kind," said Titch. "Smallish, dark brown mottled with white."

"Speckled Woods," Crusoe told him. "Don't you know the names of butterflies, then?" He sounded quite surprised.

Michael said he knew a Red Admiral and a Tortoishell, but that was about all.

"Quite time you were educated then!" said Crusoe laughing. "I think I've got a book up there"—he pointed to the shelf on the wall behind Titch's head—"but let's clear away and get rid of this crockery first of all." He closed Michael's Nature Log Book and gave it back to him. "Grand piece of work," he said. "I think that's much the most satisfactory way of collecting things."

"It's all right if you're clever at drawing," grumbled Titch, piling the plates together. "I couldn't do anything like that."

"You're just too lazy to try," Crusoe retorted.

Titch shook his head. "Never was any good at it," he said. "Never really bothered with collecting things, either.

Other chaps went in for cigarette cards and stamps and bus tickets and swopped them about all over the place. Waste of time, I call it."

"That's because you satisfy yourself in another way," said Crusoe. "What *did* you do in your spare time?"

"Practised in the gym, mostly," Titch answered.

"Well, there you are. Takes all sorts to make a world and you're not a collector."

"I don't mind using my hands," said Titch. "But not finicking about with pencils and brushes. I like carpentry. I like making things; solid things."

"Here's a chance for you to use your hands right now," said Crusoe, staggering down the steps with a pile of dirty crocks. "Grand sunny morning—we'll wash-up outside again."

Titch was soon wielding the mop and keeping Crusoe and Michael busy drying things. The mist had disappeared; the grass was a plain, dry green; no longer softened by dew. Prince the carthorse was enjoying his morning feed of oats and hay round behind the caravan; they could hear his contented munching.

"I'll have to give him some work to do soon," Crusoe said, polishing a glass till it sparkled in the sunshine. "He'll be so full of beans I won't be able to manage him."

"Let's go off somewhere when Derek and Diana come," Michael suggested. "Can you take the waggon through the forest?"

"There is a track . . ." Crusoe began, but the sound of hoofbeats across on the road made up look up. Prince gave a muffled whinny, greeting a fellow-quadruped, as a pony and trap came into view, trotting down the rise from Dalehurst. The road forked at that point; one way leading up quite steeply into the trees; the other curving round the open space of grass and running in front of the white-washed walls of the inn.

". . . track I think we could use," Crusoe continued. "We could make our way right across the forest to the west." He broke off, and with Michael and Titch, stared across to the road again. "We'll see how the D.'s feel when they come. We might make a start to-morrow."

"What's the matter with the little horse?" Titch asked, his sleeves rolled up and his hands white with froth.

"Just what I was wondering," said Crusoe.

"I've seen that pony and trap before," said Michael. "Going into Dalehurst yesterday, when I was waiting for Titch. An oldish lady was driving and the pony seemed quiet enough then."

"Not so quiet now," said Titch. "Looks as if there's a bunch of kids aboard. Don't think they'll do any good with that whip."

Crusoe shook his head. "Nor do I," he said. "I hate to see a pony treated like that. Must be something wrong, for it to refuse the hill."

"Let's go across," pressed Michael. "Do let's try and stop them."

Titch had already wiped his hands on one of the dishcloths. "Coming?" he asked.

"I think we'd better," said Crusoe reluctantly, and led the way across the green.

The sound of furious argument came to their ears long before they reached the trap; it's occupants seemed to be disagreeing with each other at the top of their shrill voices. The pony was rearing and backing and grew more and more restive, the more punishment it received. There were two girls and a boy in the trap, Michael saw as they came nearer, and the boy held the reins and was shouting furiously at the pony and slashing it with his whip. One of the girls, she had red hair he noticed, was shouting just as angrily and was trying to stop the boy by force, but the other girl was holding her back. They were all of them in a savage temper and at the moment the pony and the girl with red hair seemed to be getting the worst of it. What a jolly party! Michael thought as they came running up.

"Philip, stop it! I tell you stop it! Let me go, Margaret, can't you! You're not to . . ." The red-haired girl was nearly in tears.

"I'll teach you! Get on, can't you! Get on!" The boy was shouting at the pony, his face very flushed.

"What's all the trouble about?" Crusoe's level voice cut across the pandemonium. In the general excitement none of the children had seen the approach of the campers. There was a moment's pause. Then the boy and the girl with red hair spoke almost simultaneously.

"Nothing to do with you," the one growled and flourished the whip.

"Oh, please stop him," cried the girl. "They won't let me . . . He's beastly, I *hate* him. I hate you both. You won't ever stay with me or drive Puck again, never, never, *never!*"

"Steady a moment," said Crusoe, stepping across to the pony's head. He tried to lead him forward, but the cob refused until Crusoe pulled him half round at an angle to the slope. "You haven't got your traces even," he said. "You're rubbing a sore on his flank. You can't expect him to pull as you've fixed 'em now. And go easy with the whip another time. I wouldn't trust you with a horse until you'd learnt to control yourself better."

He made the traces even and then found a pair of earnest eyes staring down at him from the trap.

"Thank you," said the little girl with red hair. "I knew there must be something the matter, because Puck was always as quiet as anything when I went out before. Only Philip wouldn't stop and listen to me."

The boy was glowering; his face set in sulky lines. He had not said anything or made a move since Crusoe took charge. The other girl in the trap, podgy, with a round, blank face, looked at him stolidly and remained silent, too.

"That's all right," said Crusoe. "Why don't you drive now, for a change. I think you'll find he'll take the hill."

The little girl shook her head doubtfully.

"She's not allowed to," said the boy abruptly. "In case anything happened. She's not strong enough." His voice held the faintest suspicion of a sneer.

"I'm sorry," said Crusoe. "I didn't realize . . ." And he turned back and joined Titch and Michael, who were standing by the roadside.

For the first time, the little girl saw them all three together; saw behind them, in the distance, the green and red painted waggon and the tent by the trees.

"Is that where you live?" she asked, a sudden interest transforming her thin face. "Is that your caravan?"

Crusoe nodded; unprepared for the next question.

"Are you Mr. Robinson?" As he nodded again, she rushed on breathlessly. "Where are Derek and Diana? I expect they've told you about me. I'm Cynthia Crawley."

His blank, astonished expression told her something was wrong. "You did say you were Mr. Robinson? You're called Crusoe? Then haven't you met Diana and her brother? They stayed with us the night before last and went off yesterday. They were going to find you at the Royal Oak."

"Derek and Diana! No, they never came here," said Crusoe. "I wasn't expecting them till to-day. How on earth . . ."

"No, they were meeting you in the forest," Cynthia insisted. "At the Royal Oak. You know, the biggest tree of all. That's where you told them you'd be. Derek knew where it was, he had a guide book with a photo of it, so he knew what it looked like."

"But . . . but . . ." stammered Crusoe, turning and pointing to the whitewashed inn across the green; the painted sign hanging over the door. "*That*'s the Royal Oak I meant. I've been here all the time."

And Cynthia and the man she had heard so much about stared at each other with growing astonishment and concern.

CHAPTER 13

Two Birds with a Stone

MICHAEL pulled the groundsheet outside the tent and arranged himself comfortably. He had borrowed a cushion from the caravan, and around him spread everything he was likely to need. Water in a potted-meat jar; brushes; his paintbox and the extra tubes; pencils; indiarubber; bird book opened at the illustration of a long-tailed tit, and, of course, his Nature Log. He was all set for work. Everything was quiet; the sun was pleasantly warm and shone down from a clear sky; the tree tops behind him might have been made of burnished gold, each twig gleaming against the deep blue. The weather was perfect and hinted of summer; yet there was a freshness and vigour in the air that was very different from the hot, lazy-making hours of July and August. The forest; the stretch of green grass; the strip of road where purred and buzzed an occasional car; the white blocks of the inn buildings—yes, it was all very nice, or would have been, perhaps, on some other morning as fine as this.

Michael fiddled about with his brushes; mixed a pale brown and began work on his sketch of the tits' nest. But he soon found that he was not concentrating. He kept on looking up; his eyes straying across the green to where the road curved towards Dalehurst. Titch and Crusoe had gone off on bicycles; the children following in their pony cart. They had disappeared down that stretch of road—oh, a long time ago now. There was nothing he could do. "You stay here and keep an eye on things, Michael," Crusoe had said, before pedalling off with Titch as if they were competing in some race. Everything was quiet; he was quite alone. But—were they coming back yet? Had they found them? What had happened to Derek and Diana? Where had they been; what had they been doing all this time?

Funny, that a complete stranger, the little girl with red hair, should have known Crusoe's name; should have recognized him like that! And not only Crusoe! She had asked which of them was called Titch. "Derek's found your knife," she had said. "We went to the gypsies' camp yesterday morning, but they'd gone before we got there." "I went back to the camp, too," Titch had replied. "I saw a couple of kids pushing a pram." And it was them! He had actually *seen* the D.'s!

Michael had never known Crusoe so worried before. "Where is this oak?" he had asked. "We'd better go at once. The quicker the better." "They won't be there, now," the little girl had said. "Derek was sure you'd all be travelling with the gypsies, and they're going down to the coast. I expect he'll try and follow after them."

But Crusoe decided not to chance it. He found out the best way to reach the Royal Oak; asked the girl where she lived and arranged to come to her house afterwards if their search was unsuccessful. "I'd like a word with your father. I'm not at all clear how this has happened," he had said. "They never told me they were coming as soon as this."

Michael rinsed his brush absent-mindedly and stared at the little jar of cloudy water. Somewhere, miles away perhaps, Derek and Diana were searching for Crusoe; growing more and more desperate as time went on and they found no trace or sign of him anywhere. Here, by contrast, everything was quiet and safe; the sunlight warm on the green-painted sides, the red spokes of the caravan.

And he, Michael, was lazing about, sketching, with nothing better to do!

He drew out the brush, noticing with almost unconscious approval the way the hairs came together into a fine point as the water drained away. They were good sable paintbrushes, the best kind of all. Daddy himself had given them to him, last Christmas. He hovered over the colours, uncertain where to begin next. The pale grey-green of the lichen and dried moss would be a difficult shade; perhaps if he mixed . . . He looked up suddenly, for no apparent reason, and there was Titch, riding one bicycle and leading another, pedalling over the rough grass towards him.

Michael was on his feet in an instant. The jar of water fell over, but he never noticed. "Have you found them?" he shouted, running to meet his brother.

Titch shook his head. "No luck," he grunted. "We didn't expect to see them, but we know they went there yesterday afternoon. We came back by some plantations and one of the men remembered telling them how to get to the Royal Oak."

"You've been ages," said Michael. "Where's Crusoe? At the girl's house?"

Titch handed him his bicycle. "Yes," he said. "We ran into the most frightful schimozzle. The whole family were running amok."

"What, about the D.'s?" asked Michael.

"No, nothing to do with them. A fat old lady was having hysterics and it was taking everyone all their time to pull her round. Something about the gypsies and her savings, I couldn't make head or tail of it. Crusoe sent me to fetch you, because we're going down to the coast."

"Wait while I put my things away. Oh, *bother!*" Michael began mopping furiously with his handkerchief. "Water's gone all over the page."

"Come on," said Titch impatiently. "Can't wait all day."

"But I'm *smudging* it," wailed Michael.

"Leave it to dry, fathead, and clean it up afterwards."

Michael put his Log Book inside the tent and took a last glance at the blotched page. "I must have knocked the jar over," he said. "I've made an awful mess."

"D'you know," Titch remarked as they rode off together, "the red-haired girl's a cripple. She was going about in the house with crutches and iron things on her legs."

"Um!" said Michael, still thinking of his spoilt masterpiece.

"Rotten luck, that," Titch continued. "She was sitting in the trap before, so of course we didn't notice anything wrong."

"The boy said she wasn't strong enough to drive. Don't you remember?"

"So he did," said Titch. "Nasty little beast that. Needs stepping on."

"Titch, how are we going to the coast? We've only got two bicycles."

"You're driving in the trap with the old man," Titch explained. "Of course, I *knew* there was something I hadn't told you! The girl's father is the man I met in the wood. You know, who stopped me fighting with the gypsy."

Michael thought it all out. "I suppose Derek knew him," he said. "Queer thing that we should . . ."

"No, he didn't. Not from Adam!" Titch chuckled.

By this time they were threading their way through the main shopping street of Dalehurst. "They bluffed a night's lodging by pretending to be the boy and girl we saw in the trap. Evidently the old lady's doing. I'm not sure how it all happened, but it sounded a good lark."

"Doesn't sound a bit like the D.'s," said Michael doubtfully. "I suppose it *was* them."

"Certain," said Titch. "Derek recognized my knife. Couldn't be anyone else."

Michael was still in a daze. "How did they manage . . ."

"Keep your eye on the road," warned Titch. "Too much traffic for day dreaming."

"But, Titch," said Michael, catching him up and riding abreast again outside the town. "Why are these people driving down to the coast, too? Are they helping us to find the D.'s?"

"Partly that," said Titch. "But it's mostly to do with this trouble of the old lady's! Some gypsy woman's got hold of her savings and we're going to try and get the money back for her." They were pedalling furiously down the long, steady slope from Dalehurst and Titch had to shout in jerky sentences; his words blown back by the wind. "As far as I can gather—you can't help laughing, really—a gypsy fortune-teller's hoaxed the old girl—told her that if she let her bury the money and say spells over it, the money would double itself in a few months. Can you believe it?"

"Sounds like a fairy story!" said Michael. "And she did?"

"Course she did!" bawled Titch. "And now she finds she's lost the whole packet! What d'you expect?"

Michael was too much out of breath to answer and his head, anyway, was all in a whirl.

They arrived, at last, at the Crawley's house and found
Crusoe standing in the drive by the pony cart, talking
to Mr. Crawley. They were discussing the theft of Mrs.
Potts' savings.

"It's a clear case of *Hokano Baro*," the old man was
saying, as if he were a doctor diagnosing a serious com-
plaint. "Mind you, the trick is as old as the hills, but
while there are credulous people—I was going to say
fools—in the world, they'll get away with it. What *does*
surprise me is that they dared come into my own household. I am not unknown to the Romany tribes in this
part of the country and would have put a stop to any
such nonsense if I had had the slightest suspicion what
was going on. As it is, we have a very serious matter to
deal with and in view of my reputation, shall we say,
among the gypsies, I hesitate to call in the police. Not
that they would be very effective in this case," he added
as an afterthought.

"What is this trick?" Crusoe asked. "I'm still completely
in the dark."

"*Hokano Baro!* A form of confidence trick, I suppose
you'd call it. An old favourite among gypsies all over the
world. The idea is to convince some gullible person that
their house or garden contains buried treasure. They'll
quote historical and other far-fetched evidence; spin the
most astonishing yarns. And this treasure will only come
to light if another lot of valuables is buried nearby, to
which it will be magically attracted. All moonshine, of
course, but you know what some people are. They'll
swallow anything from a gypsy with the gift of the
gab!"

"Don't quite see how they work it, yet," said Crusoe.
"What happens then?" Titch and Michael came up and

stood silently by while Mr. Crawley continued his explanation.

"Once they've hooked their fish, the rest's easy. The hoard is buried, in this case Mrs. Potts' savings for the past few years, and I expect the gypsy muttered magic spells over it and swore her to secrecy. They'll usually tell you that the magic treasure will grow less, the more it is talked about. On her second visit, the fortune-teller will bring hidden under her cloak a bundle similar to the bag of money and plate she has buried, and the two are secretly exchanged. The victim of the hoax is, of course, told on no account to disturb the treasure for at least three weeks or the spell will be broken. This gives time enough for the gypsies to disappear into the blue. And when the weeks are up and the cellar or hole is searched, not two treasures, not even the original hoard is found, but only a bag of old rubbish!"

Crusoe slowly nodded. "Very clever," he said. "Very clever indeed. But the gypsies have only been gone a day or two. How did you manage to discover the fraud so soon?"

"Mrs. Potts is not a naturally silent person," Mr. Crawley replied. "She told my daughter Cynthia about her remarkable prospects and Cynthia had the good sense to tell me. I investigated, of course, with the result that Mrs. Potts now appears to be permanently incapacitated and her recovery to good health and spirits will depend largely on our efforts." He smiled at Crusoe and there was a twinkle in his eye, despite his serious expression. "But here are your friends, back again. I've been wasting your time with all this talk, and you have more serious troubles of your own. I shall be only too glad to help you in your inquiries about these missing children.

I've no doubt they'll turn up safe and sound—a charming pair. I was deceived at first into thinking my sister's children had made a remarkable improvement in manners . . ." Mr. Crawley sighed. "I'm afraid my hopes were not fulfilled. If you're ready, then, let us start at once. But what's all this? Mrs. Potts appears to have risen from her bed of sickness!"

"Oh, sir! Oh, sir!" cried this lady, coming down the steps from the front door in a tremendous flurry. "Miss Cynthia's just been telling me 'bout them poor children, and I'm that worried I couldn't stay quiet and rest. This is the gentleman, sir?" she asked Mr. Crawley, indicating Crusoe. "Deary me, all these 'appenings one after the other fair makes my head swim. The poor mites! When I brought them in out of the rain, I thought to myself . . ."

"Yes, yes, quite so, Mrs. Potts," said Mr. Crawley soothingly. "And Mr. Robinson's very grateful for the help we were able to give them. We're just this moment about to start."

"Oh, sir, if you bring them two children back safe and sound, I'll never say another word about my savings. It did seem bad to me, this morning, when Mr. Crawley, he tells me I've been deceived," said Mrs. Potts earnestly, turning to Crusoe. "What little money I'd managed to put by—and I'm not the saving sort, sir—Potts, he was always at me about my careless way with what little we had. 'D'you think I'm made of money,' he used to say to me when he was alive, sir. And what bit I'd saved stolen by that gypsy woman, and after all she'd told me of the chest of treasure buried under the house! She's a wicked woman, sir, and I hope . . ."

"Now, Mrs. Potts, be charitable," said Mr. Crawley,

raising a hand. "If I'm not very much mistaken you shall have your money back to-day, and I hope you'll take my advice after this and bank it!"

But Mrs. Potts was not so easily stopped. "There's them that'll call me foolish for listening and believing such a story, but I can tell you, sir, she was that persuasive she'd 'ave convinced anybody. 'Can't you sense the gold in this house?' she says to me—I can feel her black, gleaming eyes on me now, like a snake if only I'd known it. A snake in the grass! And the way she mouthed out 'gold!' I could feel the weight of the sovereigns, sir. 'Like attracts like!' she tells me. 'Treasure to treasure all the wide world over!' And she tells me, confidential, what she's done for other ladies, sir, and how little they gave her for it. 'I hope you'll be more generous,' she whines at me. 'You've a kind face.'" And Mrs. Potts shook her fist in rage.

Mr. Crawley took her firmly by the arm and led her up the front steps, while Crusoe, Titch and Michael waited by the pony cart. They caught a glimpse of a pale face watching them from one of the windows.

"The cripple girl," said Titch, and waved and grinned cheerily. He was naturally kind-hearted and felt for Cynthia Crawley as he had felt for a bird with a broken wing, brought home and nursed on board the houseboat *Sally* over a year ago.

Crusoe ran his fingers through his hair. "What a morning," he said, half to himself. "I'm beginning to feel like Mrs. Potts!"

"When are we going to start?" Michael asked impatiently.

"Right now," said Crusoe. "Mr. Crawley thinks he can trail the gypsies, but they've got a day's start of us, so we'll have to keep moving. And where the gypsies are, *we* hope we'll find Derek and Diana, and *he* hopes to get back Mrs. Potts' savings, so we've our work cut out."

"Busy day ahead," said Titch, waving again. "Two birds with one stone!"

Mr. Crawley came down from the house at that moment, and gathering the reins in his gloved hands, mounted the trap.

"Up you get," he said to Michael, who lost no time in seating himself beside the old gentleman.

Crusoe and Titch swung into their saddles and pedalled slowly after them as they turned through the driveway gates. Breaking into a steady trot, they were soon spanking along the open highway between the low hedges; meeting the fresh breeze and feeling the sun warm on their faces; off on the chase at last on a fine spring morning; the countryside spreading out on either hand under the blue bowl of the sky.

CHAPTER 14

Poacher's Stew

"CAREFUL!" Mr. Crawley shouted from the trap, as Crusoe and Titch, tumbling off their bicycles, ran across to the heap of white ashes by the roadside. "Don't go and burn your hands! We may be closer to them than we think." He gave the reins to Michael to hold and climbed stiffly down. "I remember I plunged my hands into some ashes once, to see how warm they were—and the party had only moved on that same morning. I was bandaged up for a week!" He crossed to the remains of the camp fire and joined the others, kneeling on the ground.

"Let's see," he murmured, gently brushing the ashes with a stick and holding his hand, palm flat, close above them. "I thought as much. Feel." And Crusoe had to admit that he would have burnt himself. "But this is not the main camp." Mr. Crawley was looking around the strip of grass; examining the hedge. There was something rather incongruous in the sight of this respectable, carefully dressed old man nosing about by the roadside, for all the world like a dog after a rabbit. But Crusoe and the Crosbie brothers watched him without a smile. They had already, this morning, followed in his footsteps like a trio of admiring Dr. Watsons dogging their Sherlock Holmes. No sign was too small; no indication, however slight, had been missed, the whole, long way from Dalehurst.

The low, overhanging branches of a tree, perhaps, were bent and snapped; a clear sign that waggons had passed by. From his seat high up in the trap, Mr. Crawley would point to a couple of twigs lying one on top of the other by the edge of the road; the longer stick indicating the way the gypsies had taken. Or perhaps it was a twist of grass or a forked spray of hawthorn from the hedge. However small, Mr. Crawley invariably noticed these indications (*patterans* he called them) placed by the gypsies for others of their tribe to read and follow.

They had already left the high-road and were lost in a maze of tiny lanes and byways; but they were on the trail, right enough. Villagers in the hamlet they had just passed remembered the waggons creaking through, early in the morning, with the first half-light. But Derek and Diana? Crusoe was wondering. How could they have possibly hoped to catch up with the gypsies? As time passed and the sun began to drop towards the west, he grew more and more anxious. They could never have threaded their way through this network of roads! True, they were heading south, towards the coast, but that was a vague, general direction and of very little help.

"This is not the main camp," Mr. Crawley repeated. "I should imagine the waggons are straggling, by this time, and that some are getting left behind the rest. If we press on quickly, we shall catch up with the rearguard before very much longer."

Greatly cheered, Crusoe and Titch mounted their bicycles again and pony and trap trotted off along the road. And even Mr. Crawley was surprised how soon his prophecy was to be fulfilled.

"Waggon ahead!" shouted Titch, after they had covered another mile or so. He was spinning down a short hill and had taken the lead. Half hidden as yet, round the bend at the foot of the slope, he saw the back of a caravan.

Crusoe pedalled after him and together they came up with the waggon; to find that it was stationary, pulled well into the side of the road. The scrawny old horse was nibbling at the shoots of green grass growing on the bank below the hedge. The derelict appearance of the faded, dirty paintwork told it's own story. Titch and Crusoe both recognized the caravan and looked around everywhere for it's owner; but there was no sign of the little gypsy.

Mr. Crawley drew up the cob behind them and Crusoe went across, leaving his bicycle propped against a wheel. "This is Patch Cooper's waggon," he explained. "An old friend of ours. He doesn't seem to be about anywhere, I'm afraid."

"What's he doing? Why has he left his caravan here?" Michael wanted to know. "Perhaps his harness has broken again. D'you think so?"

But Mr. Crawley had another idea.

"I'll wager he's out after rabbits," he said. "I know the man, too. An inveterate poacher if there ever was one!"

Crusoe grinned; remembering the trouble this weakness of his had caused them, the previous summer holidays.

"Shall we wait for him?" he asked. "He might be able to help us."

Mr. Crawley climbed down from the trap and, walking past the caravan, slapped the neck of the gypsy's skinny horse. Carefully, he felt round the collar.

"Sweat's dry," he said. "We shouldn't have to stay long. He's not going to risk anything, and a parked caravan is a conspicuous object in a quiet lane like this."

"Here he comes!" cried Titch at that moment, as if in answer.

"He hasn't had any luck," said Michael, quite disappointed.

They all gazed down the road as the little, squat figure of Patch Cooper came striding towards them. He seemed shorter and thicker than ever; his brown velveteen trousers crumpled and absurdly baggy. The cap was set on his head at the same old angle, and at his heels pattered the inevitable, pale-coloured, meekly-fawning pup. But, as Michael had noticed, his hands were empty and he carried no bulging sack across his shoulders.

"Good afternoon to you, gentlemen!" he exclaimed, coming up to them; his dark face all one smile of surprise. "I was thinking I'd left you many a mile behind me! Howsoever, you're the more welcome. I see you've got your *chavies* with you, safe and sound, Mr. Robinson."

"*What!*" Crusoe exclaimed, not quite following him. "Oh yes, of course. Titch and Michael! I thought for the moment . . ."

"Now, look here, Cooper," said Mr. Crawley in a very businesslike way. "We're not out for an afternoon's jaunt. We've serious matters to discuss with you. I think you'd better put those rabbits of yours away and then we can . . ."

"*Rabbits!*" Michael said to himself incredulously. What was Mr. Crawley talking about? But the little gypsy never batted an eyelid. If anything, his face wrinkled appreciatively, and he nodded and slapped his hands on his thighs.

"No good tryin' to pull the skin over *your* eyes, Mr. Crawley," he said. "It'll be an unhappy day for a good many of us when you turn gamekeeper!"

Mr. Crawley snorted. "At my age!" he said. "Don't be ridiculous, man!"

Crusoe, who was standing next to Patch Cooper, stooped and felt his crumpled, velveteen trousers. He was grinning when he unbent himself.

"He's got a rabbit slung each side of his legs," he told Titch and Michael.

"I *thought* his trousers looked jolly baggy," said Michael, "but I never . . ."

The gypsy treated them to a slow wink.

"So you wants to talk serious-like," he said, turning to Mr. Crawley. "I won't keep you waiting a minute." And he creaked up the steps into the caravan.

"Now, Cooper," said Mr. Crawley briskly, when he joined them again a moment or two later. "Mr. Robinson here has lost a couple of his children. Er—what were their names?"

"Derek and Diana, the Longmores. You met them last summer," Crusoe explained. "I expect you remember. They're on their own somewhere, trying to follow you all down to the coast. They think I'm travelling along with you. Have you seen them at all, or heard anything about them?"

Patch Cooper shook his head. "I know the *chavies* you mean," he said. "No, I haven't set eyes on 'em, but you can trust me to keep a sharp look out. How long have they been missing, then?"

"Since yesterday lunch-time," said Mr. Crawley. "They left my house and disappeared into the blue. They mistook Mr. Robinson's instructions and went to the wrong place to meet him. He wasn't expecting them till to-day."

The little gypsy looked grave. "That's bad," he said. "They're too young to be wandering on their own. I'm thinking the *muskeros* should be able to help you."

"We've let them know, of course," said Mr. Crawley. "You gave the police a description, didn't you?" he asked Crusoe.

" 'Phoned them from your house," said Crusoe. "I'll make some inquiries, the next town we come to."

"Now, the other question," Mr. Crawley continued,

"concerns a very different matter. I don't think I need explain to you the practice of *Hokano baro?*"

Patch Cooper's brown face gave nothing away. His black eyes narrowed a little and he met Mr. Crawley's gaze without blinking.

"I've a housekeeper, Mrs. Potts by name—who has been in the family for years. She looks after my daughter Cynthia, who needs especial care, as of course you know. I discovered, only this morning, that she had lost the whole of her savings to a fortune-teller, presumably from your camp below my house. This woman practised the fraud under my own roof!" Mr. Crawley's voice rose a little with suppressed anger. "Naturally I am not going to let this pass. I intend to find her and demand the return of the money. Knowing your people as well as I do, over a long period of years, I must say that I am bitterly disappointed. Always before I have been treated with scrupulous fairness and courtesy."

The little gypsy nodded slowly; his face frowning and serious. "Aye, that's bad. That's bad," he murmured. "And I haven't a doubt . . ."

"As far as I can gather, she was quite a young woman," Mr. Crawley continued. "Black hair down to her shoulders, tied with pieces of ribbon; large gold ear-rings; bright-coloured clothes and a long cloak."

"That's her!" The gypsy nodded again. "She's a wild, headstrong girl and knows her power. Mr. Crawley, you want to be careful what you're doing. There's a rough lot of young men and women joined us; from the North they've come and brought wanton new ways with them. Lavinia Ayres, she's Levi's wife, and Levi is a hot-blooded man as your young friend here will swear to, knowing him well." And he pointed to Titch with a quick gesture of his hand. "If you press her, she'll know nothing about *Hokano baro*, bless her lily-white, innocent heart. You won't get no change out of her, mark my words. As I said, them lot are new to this part of the country and don't know you and won't stand on ceremony, I'll be bound."

Mr. Crawley hesitated. "What do you advise, then?" he asked. "I've no wish, whatsoever, to bring in . . ."

"And no good they'd do, neither," snapped the gypsy, guessing what was to come. "Where's your proof? She'll know nothing of it, and where are you?"

"Very much what I thought, myself," said Mr. Crawley. "In fact, I'd ruled out the police and was hoping to achieve a settlement myself."

"You won't achieve nothing with that set of rough-toughs," said the little gypsy decisively. " 'Cept, maybe, a fist in your face or a bottle across your head, to serve you for meddling." He stood for a moment, gazing down at the roadway between his boots, thinking things over. "You'd best leave it to me," he said at last. "It's a small chance, maybe, but worth taking. Aye, you'd best leave it to Patch Cooper!"

"What, then . . ."

"Two miles along this road, turn right. 'Nother ten miles, maybe a stretch more, brings you to Dareham, and that's where we'll be finding the party we wants to-night. But don't you go as far as the town. You'll pass an inn on top of a hill 'bout one mile short of Dareham—you can see the church tower down in the fold of the valley. You put up there—you'll find stabling for your pony—and wait till I come. Maybe you'll not see me till after dark."

"But can't we . . ."

"You'll help me best by staying right out o' the town till I wants you," said the little gypsy. "I'll make a few inquiries in my own way, first, and then we'll see better how we stand."

"It's really very good of you . . ."

"Mr. Crawley, none of that. This never ought to have happened, and if Patch Cooper can make matters square with you, he will, right enough. And now, before we start off, what would you gentlemen say to a bite of something to eat?"

"Well!" said Mr. Crawley, looking round at the others, "we haven't stopped for refreshment since we started. Have we time, do you think?"

"Time enough and to spare," said Patch Cooper. "You're faster travellers than I am and there's not much I can do before evening. I'll stir the fire in the range a moment. Won't you seat yourselves on the grass by the hedge?"

He disappeared and they heard the grating noise of a riddler; saw a column of smoke rise from the blackened stump of a chimney, jutting at a crazy angle from the roof of the gypsy's waggon.

"I suppose this *is* all right," sighed Mr. Crawley as, spreading the rug from the trap, they settled themselves by the roadside. "I must say, I'd much prefer to try my own hand at the game."

"I really don't think it would be advisable," said Crusoe. "At least, let's give Patch a chance to do his stuff. He hasn't let us down yet."

"He's a good fellow," agreed Mr. Crawley. "One of the best, in spite of his poaching. The rascal! I could have seen those rabbits of his a mile away. He's not long enough in the leg." And the old man chuckled quietly; stretching himself and looking around him. "We couldn't have asked for finer weather," he said. "The spring makes the blood flow quicker even in my old veins!"

"I wonder what he means to do?" Michael whispered to Titch. "I should love to know what he's planning."

"Secretive old chap," Titch said. "I think he rather enjoys being mysterious. Remember what Derek said about him, last summer? When he went off with Pam and Diana to buy Crusoe's caravan?"

"Levi was the man you had the fight with?"

Titch nodded. "Last time we saw him he was dancing around like a scalded cat."

"He *was* a scalded cat," said Michael. "And his wife is the fortune-teller?"

Titch nodded again. "Nice pair," he grunted. "I only wish I was stronger! Hullo, here's the old boy with his basket of crocks. Go and bring it across for him Mike, there's a sport."

Michael obediently fetched the hamper and before they had time to lay out the knives and plates and cut slices off the loaf they found inside, Patch Cooper was back again with his black pot swinging beside him.

"I always has a pot on the fire," he said, seating himself beside them. "Though, mind you, I'm not much in the way of a cook. I hopes this will be to your liking."

He lifted the lid and a savoury steam wafted under the noses of the hungry travellers. Mr. Crawley gave one sniff and stared fixedly at the swarthy little man who, with complete unconcern, was dishing out from his hot-pot on to the row of plates. He did not open his mouth to speak, however, until his helping had been passed to him and he had taken a first, appreciative mouthful. Then the old man looked up and shook his head, reprovingly.

"Cooper!" he exclaimed. "I've said it before and I shall say it again. You're a rascal! One of these days you'll go to prison and expect me to bail you out. This is extremely nice pheasant . . ."

CHAPTER 15

Fun at the Fair!

"This is ridiculous!" stormed Mr. Crawley, pacing up and down between the trestle table and the fireplace. "We can't wait about like this and waste our time. How long have we been here? Three hours . . . four . . . ? And what about those children of yours, eh, Robinson? We're no nearer to *them!*"

Crusoe, sitting on the edge of a wheel-backed chair, his hands cupping his chin, nodded silently. The hearth was blank and cold; the room growing thick with shadow as the light faded outside the one square window. The walls were papered with cards, red and white and deep blue; prizes for pigs, First, Seconds and Thirds, at the local agricultural show. A photograph in a gilt frame over the mantelpiece showed the largest and finest sow of them all, Champion Bessie, distended like a toy balloon. Michael and Titch were stretching their legs under the table, perched on a slippery bench, their backs against the wall. They wore the fixed, glazed look of boys enduring the dullest class of the week.

"Stick another penny in, for goodness sake, Mike!" said Titch. "I can't just sit here and listen to myself breathing."

"It'll be the *Isle of Capri* again," Michael warned him, but Titch was past caring. In the corner by the door stood a species of barrel-organ, glorified into an imitation piano with an ornamented, fretwork case. Michael pressed a penny into the slot. The machine digested the coin with a hiccough and, as he turned the handle at the end, groaned and wheezed in dire torment. A few jangling,

twanging notes tumbled over each other; the crowd
thickened into discord; for a moment confusion reigned
and then the notes sorted themselves out into the thump-
ing, funereal procession of the dance tune.

Jingle-twang-jingle-twang-twonka-punka . . .

"Faster!" said Titch, leaning back dreamily and
beating time with his hand. "Faster!"

Michael did his best to accelerate, but the handle was
stiff and hard to turn.

Pinka-ponk-pinka-ponk-pinka-ponk . . .

"No more after this, please!" shouted Crusoe above
the din. "Can't you make it play something else?"

"We've heard all four tunes twice, now," panted
Michael. "This is our last penny."

"On the Isle of Capri that I met her . . ." Titch sang
lustily, nearly drowning the barrel-organ.

"Thank goodness for that," said Crusoe, relapsing
again with his chin on his hands.

"Father says——" repeated the little girl, who had come
into the room unnoticed. "Will you be wanting supper
and when would you like it?"

"Supper!" cried Mr. Crawley. "Supper! Is that how
late it is? Stop that confounded din, boy. What *is* the
time? . . ."

Pin-ka-ponk. The music slurred into silence. The little
girl in the doorway regarded them all with wide eyes.
She moistened her lips with her tongue and waited for
an answer. She looked as wound up as a clockwork toy;
needing only a word to send her flying off again into the
mysterious confines of the inn.

"Supper!" Mr. Crawley repeated again. "How much
longer! Seven o'clock and not a sign . . ."

"Let's order our meal for eight o'clock and have a

quick look round by ourselves, first," said Crusoe. "I *must* make some inquiries."

Mr. Crawley thought this an excellent idea.

"Supper for four, then, at eight o'clock," he said. "Meanwhile we'll go down to Dareham. What can you manage? Cold ham or beef? Pickles? Bread and cheese?"

The landlord's daughter said she'd see what father could do. "Harry's just come back from the Fair," she added, before closing the door behind her. "Won a statue, he has. All gold. We've put it on the mantelpiece."

Mr. Crawley and Crusoe stared at each other. "*Fair!*" cried Titch, but the little girl had gone.

"Cooper never mentioned a fair," said Mr. Crawley. "He must have known. We should have investigated before this!"

"You think the gypsies . . ."

"Why, of course! We mustn't lose a minute!" Mr. Crawley reached for his hat and coat, and a few seconds later the door of the inn opened and disgorged four travellers, who set off, walking briskly, down the deserted road.

The dusk had thickened; the small town below them in the valley was a mass of twinkling lights; a handful of brilliant dust thrown down carelessly on the dim folds of the countryside. One patch of lights was brighter than the rest and as they descended, drawing rapidly nearer the houses, they began to hear fragments of blaring music; shouts and cries muffled by distance; a whisper as yet of all the fun of the fair!

"This is something like!" Titch exclaimed, as at last they found their way through the dark streets and came out opposite an archway of coloured light; the entrance to the fairground.

The field was thronged. Every lane between the rows of

stalls and sideshows was crowded; the people there brilliantly lit in the glare of electric lamps. Heaped prizes glittered before the shooting-ranges; the ninepins; the dartboards and games of chance. Cut glass, gaudy vases, gilt statues like the one Harry (whoever he might be) had brought triumphantly back with him to the inn, earlier that day, were all displayed; an astounding and colourful array, guaranteed to tempt the procession of onlookers to try their skill.

Titch had already grabbed three wooden balls and was taking his stance before the white ninepins.

"Try your luck, sir! Try your luck! Knock down four out of five to win!"

Michael watched his brother throw, aiming at the tower; five ninepins balanced one on top of the other. The top of the second one up; that was the key point. A ball smack there would bring four tumbling down for a prize. The bases were heavily weighted; you had to hit the tops to knock them off the stand.

Titch hurled with all his strength and the first ball thudded into the canvas at the back of the booth. His second went straight, but high, and flicked off the topmost ninepin of all. Three more to down and only one more ball! Titch threw—and missed.

"Come on! Mustn't lose the others," said Michael, as Titch turned away from the stall, angry with himself for not doing better.

They followed Crusoe and Mr. Crawley as best they could; jostling through the crowd and turning all the time to look, first on one side, then on the other. *Merryman's Marine Monsters* flared a placard in huge letters over one of the larger tents. *Man Fights Shark Under Water! Unique Spectacle! Only Show of its Kind in the World.*

"Oh, Titch!" breathed Michael. They both paused and gazed up at the dramatic paintings that lined the canvas wall. A man was standing on a box, just by the entrance, talking, talking all the time; an endless stream of words that drew them across to him, while the crowd eddied and pressed by like a river flowing over obstructing boulders.

"One sixpence, one sixpence only to see this unique and thrilling spectacle, ladies and gentlemen. An education in itself. Sea-serpents you'd never dream existed shown in the flesh. And as a climax to this remarkable entertainment, we present a *live* man fighting a *live* shark under water. Armed only with a knife, Koko, native of the South Seas, will dive into the tank of a man-eating shark, ladies and gentlemen! This is a spectacle you *cannot afford to miss!*"

The Crosbie brothers stood longingly outside the tent. Unbeknown to them, the air was vibrant with the music of steam-organs. Roundabouts whirled; switchbacks thundered—streamers of waving, rapidly careering light. Up flew the swings till they hung poised precariously, and then swept down from the darkness with a rush of wind. Snap, snap went the rifles; *biff-ting!* as somebody banged the hammer on the Try Your Strength machine and rang the bell at the very top of the tower. All around them excited people shouted, laughed, pushed in front of the stalls. But they did not hear the rumble of the Dodg'em cars, nor the voice of the crooner wailing the charms of cowboy life on the range. The shuffle and tramp of many footsteps might have been the distant beat of a mysterious sea. Crusoe and Mr. Crawley had long ago vanished from their ken. The fairground itself grew dim as with heightened suspense they paid their sixpences and stepped forward; drawn between the tent flaps into the faint, greenish glow of the aquarium.

"*Visit the Gypsy Seer*," Mr. Crawley was at that moment murmuring to himself. "*Daughter of the Original Gypsy Lee. Fortune Telling and Palmistry*." He had stopped outside a small tent, hung with placards; the canvas painted with magic signs and symbols. "I've yet to meet one of these people who *isn't* a daughter of Gypsy Lee. I came across three of them on Epsom Downs, one Derby day."

Crusoe stopped beside him and chuckled. He had been looking around, half wondering if he would see Derek and Diana anywhere in the crowd; but the idea appeared more remote and absurd with every minute that passed. They could never have found their way as far as this; alone and unaided. He turned his attention to the fortune-teller's little square tent. Two people were waiting patiently outside, and through a crack in the badly-fitting entrance, a warm red light showed that the Gypsy Seer was busy at her work.

"D'you think this is the person you want?" Crusoe asked in a low voice.

Mr. Crawley nodded. "Quite a chance," he replied. "Worth while trying, at all events. If it is, I shall do some straight talking. I've a fair command of their language and that hasn't yet failed to impress."

He took his place at the end of the queue, and Crusoe waited, loitering by the nearby booths; hoping the interview would be successful. He remembered Titch and Michael and glanced about for them, but the crowd was so thick that it was impossible to find anyone. They would look after themselves all right, he thought, turning absently to roll some pennies down a grooved slide and watch them spin and fall on the multi-coloured, chequered board of the stall. Threepence back. He rolled again and the coins curved and settled uncertainly, bridging the divisions of the squares. A small wooden rake was drawn across, sweeping his pennies into the waiting trough, and Crusoe elbowed out, glancing as he did so at the fortune-teller's tent. Mr. Crawley was still waiting outside; but alone. When Crusoe next looked across, he had disappeared.

Titch and Michael, reeling out into the brilliant fairground (minds full of the shadowy, twisting figures of man and fish weaving their fantastic pattern in the green gloom of the tank), caught from afar the murmurs, shrill cries, the quick pulse of some fresh excitement. A crowd was gathering; a crowd that grew with every passing moment, as more and more people were drawn towards the dense centre; packed tight and buzzing as a swarm of bees. What could be the matter? What was happening? The Crosbie brothers broke surface and hurried with the rest; eager and curious. Titch, stretching up, was able to see over the heads of most of the people. A woman's shrill voice babbled incessantly; Titch could see her black ringlets move on her neck as her eyes flashed in anger. She wore some sort of head-dress and bright-coloured robes which tossed when she lifted and shook her arms. And there, imprisoned in the very centre and the object, as far as Titch could see, of the woman's anger and derision, stood Mr. Crawley, with Crusoe close beside him.

"What's the matter?" Michael asked, shut in the press and wedged between backs and arms. "I can't see a thing!"

"Don't know what's up," said Titch, but his hand gripped his brother's arm, enforcing silence. He had seen a familiar face; a man whom he knew, none other than Levi Ayres, was standing close behind the gypsy and

giving her his support. Mr. Crawley, holding his ground
with dignity, was clearly harassed and wanted to with-
draw. But that was not part of the gypsy's plan, and while
the crowd held him there she flung each taunt and gibe
openly in his face, the onlookers gaping at the unusual
spectacle they presented.

" 'Ark at 'er!" said a lady in front of Titch. "Proper
scream, ain't she! The old codger tried to be too clever.
Wouldn't be in 'is shoes, not for the world."

"Wot's he done?" came a questioning voice.

"She says he told 'er fortune telling was a pack o' lies,
that's what she says. Lot o' rubbish, he called it."

"What if it is?" came another voice.

"If he thought so, what d'you think he paid sixpence
for, stoopid! Pays 'is money and tells 'er it's rubbish!
Sauce, I calls it."

"Gettin' 'is money's worth now, I'd say!" said someone
else, and a roar of laughter followed this sally.

Titch tried to edge forward, but the crowd was too
densely packed. Somehow they *must* get through! This
scene was too awful; Crusoe and Mr. Crawley made
conspicuous in front of all these beastly people. That was
Levi's wife, of course; the woman who had diddled
Mrs. Potts. They should have taken Patch Cooper's
advice and stayed away; kept clear of trouble! Perhaps
if they backed out now; tried to slip round the edge of
the crowd, they would get closer to the centre, across on
the other side. Titch, prodding Michael to follow him,
began to worm his way through the curious, staring,
stupidly-gaping throng. As he did so there was a commo-
tion and a sudden skirmish over in the direction he was
heading for, and three or four men, cloth capped and
muffled, broke through the press of people, formed a rough

lane, and hustled Mr. Crawley and Crusoe away from the penetrating, ceaseless voice of the outraged fortune-teller.

A boy and girl, looking like hikers with rucksacks on their backs, hurried through the arch of coloured lights at the entrance to the fairground. As their pace quickened, they stared about them, to the left and right, eagerly, as if expecting to see somebody they knew.

"At *last*, Derek," said the girl thankfully. "I never thought we should get here. What a lot of people!"

"Pretty good crowd," her brother admitted. "I wonder where we shall find them?"

"Oh, I *hope* they're here. Honestly, Derek, if they're not . . ."

"We shall have to go home, that's all. We've got return halves."

"Look, there's a crowd over there. What d'you think's happening?"

"Oh, some sideshow or other. This is a big fair, isn't it?"

"Not as big as Hampstead Heath," said Diana loyally.

" 'Man fights shark under water,' " murmured Derek, attracted by the Marine Monsters. "That sounds good fun. Shall we . . ."

"Not until we've tried to find Crusoe," said Diana firmly. "The crowd's moving off. I wonder what it was all about?" She gazed absently between the stalls, watching the people dispersing; the steady, even flow of passers-by resuming normal movement along the brightly lit avenues of the fair. Then, suddenly, she started forward; her face alive with excitement. "Derek! There's Crusoe! Look, going behind that tent with a lot of other people. Quick! he's gone already." And she grabbed her brother by the arm.

Together they struck across the main current of the crowd; pushing, stumbling, murmuring frantic apologies. He had slipped between the canvas outer wall of a shooting range and the gaily striped awning of a refreshment stall, where great glass jars of vivid, greeny-yellowy lemonade stood upon the brilliant white counter. She had seen him clearly in the glaring lights before he, and the men with him, had vanished into the darkness behind the booths.

Diana plunged on between protesting merrymakers; her rucksack jamming behind her as she forced a passage.

" 'Scuse me, *please!*" she gasped, running into a dark-blue, solid mass that did not move.

"Just one moment, missie," said a deep voice miles above her. "Where d'you think you're going? All by yourselves, eh?—Why, bless me, if you aren't just the couple I've been looking for!"

And Diana, raising her eyes, gazed up at the burly, helmeted figure of a police-constable.

"You can't—you can't want *us!*" cried Diana desperately. "We've just seen our friend. He'll be gone if you don't let us . . ."

"Steady does it," said the policeman soothingly. "Not quite so fast, *if* you please." He fumbled in his pocket and drew out a little notebook. With much wetting of large fingers, he flicked through the pages. "Name o' Longmore?" he inquired. "Derek and Diana? Ages 12 and 11 respectively. Probably carrying rucksacks. Slim; boy dark, girl fair." He finished reading and looked down at them, allowing himself a placid smile.

"Yes, that's us," said Derek. "I don't know who's told you, but anyway, we're not lost. We've just seen our friend, Mr. Robinson. We were going to catch him up when you stopped us. You must let us go. We've been trying to find him for ages."

"Quite so," said the police-constable with aggravating calm. He seemed to have all evening to spare, he moved and spoke so slowly! "But a Mr. Robinson informed the County Police this morning that you were missing and gave an address in Dalehurst, to which you were to be returned. Now Dareham and Dalehurst are not the same places, by any manner of means. Do you really think your friend . . ."

"But we've *seen* him!" cried Diana, losing all patience. "You're stopping us from finding him again. We knew he'd be here with the gypsies." And she attempted to wriggle round the dark-blue pillar and escape.

A huge arm shot out and a vast hand enclosed her shoulder. "None o' that now," said the constable, calm as ever. "You just come along with me and we'll soon have you settled. Now don't cry!" he added in a gentle voice. "You won't do yourself any good. Look at your brother, now. He's being a proper little man."

Derek writhed. "Where are you going to take us?" he asked sulkily. How he *hated* this great, solid lump of stupid, unsympathetic, utterly mule-like man!

"Take you home young fellow-me-lad, in time," said the constable cheerily. "First of all we'll have a sit-down by a nice fire and maybe the Superintendent will manage a cup o' tea for you and a slice o' cake. What d'you say to that?"

And he steered his charges back through the crowded fairground; back under the gay arch of coloured lights and along the dim, lonely streets of the town, until they climbed, at last, the steps of Dareham police station and the tall, glass doors swung silently behind them, shutting them off from the world outside.

CHAPTER 16

Struggle in the Dark

PATCH COOFER was quite breathless; choking with mingled anger and excitement.

"Come along now! Double quick! Through here and out of the lights." He twisted and dodged like a cornered rabbit and then dived for a black hole between two brilliantly glaring stalls. Crusoe, with Mr. Crawley and the other gypsies, tore after him. The darkness seemed intense behind the booths and the old gentleman stumbled and nearly took a header over one of the guy ropes.

"Steady there!" the gypsy hissed. "Don't want 'em after us. You've made enough of a disturbance for one night, and I hope you'll forgive plain speaking on my part. I couldn't believe my ears when they told me who was the cause of all the shindy. You've come close to ruining our work, Mr. Crawley, and you'd have done better . . ."

"I know," said that gentleman in remarkably meek tones. "I fully realize, and please accept my apologies."

"We oughtn't to have butted in," said Crusoe, "but now we're here, can't we help?"

The little gypsy snorted. They were creeping along in the semi-darkness behind the gleaming front of the stalls; avoiding the parked motor-caravans and carefully skirting the stretched ropes and tent pegs. "We would have been through with it before this, and now the whole camp's proper roused," he grumbled. "She's a vixen, that woman, and needs a whipping."

"There was not a word of truth in all her shouting

and carrying on," murmured Mr. Crawley to Crusoe. "As soon as I made a direct reference to Mrs. Potts, she began making herself objectionable in that—that highly conspicuous manner. To answer back would have only aggravated matters."

"I'm afraid it wasn't a wise move, to tackle her openly," Crusoe admitted. "But where's Patch taking us? What are we going to do now?"

The little gypsy was talking in low tones to his bunch of followers. They had stopped at the far edge of the fairground; the row of twinkling lights gleamed in the distance, fringing the soft velvet pall of the night sky. The blare and rumble of the merry-go-rounds and Dodg'em cars sounded clearly across the intervening space.

"Titch and Michael!" Crusoe suddenly exclaimed. "Where have they got to? We've lost them completely. They'll never find . . ."

But Patch Cooper had turned towards them, and they realized that he was standing by a gateway. The fair occupied an open space immediately outside the town and, as far as they could see, the gate led into a field. The black shape of a tree could just be discerned, a short distance away from them, along the hedge.

"This way!" the gypsy whispered urgently. "I want you to stand inside the field and when the horses come across, try and keep 'em together as best you can."

The gate swung behind them, the short chain secured; one link slipped over the bent nail driven into the post. Patch Cooper and his three comrades separated, and walking off at different angles, melted into the blackness of the night. Crusoe and Mr. Crawley were left alone; puzzled, wondering what was going to happen next. Horses? Keep the horses together? The little gypsy had some plan in his mind, but had not stopped to explain. And why all this urgency; this creeping and running through the dark, unless his plan was not . . . was perhaps not . . . *What was that!*

Crusoe, suddenly keyed up, spun round and tried to face all ways at once. He had heard, above the distant noise of the fair, the unmistakable sound of softly placed footsteps; the stealthy tread of someone trying to approach, undiscovered. So they had been followed after all, in spite of the careful way Patch Cooper had doubled and twisted through the darkness! Someone was creeping towards them; waiting the final moment, the nearest possible approach, before launching himself upon them! Perhaps there were two or three! Crusoe strained his eyes; his fingers itching to tear aside the veil of the night. Oh, to be able to see! To see! The quiet footsteps, carefully muffled, hesitated and stopped. Crusoe made out, or seemed to make out, a shadowy mass a shade darker than the surrounding night. He stared fixedly, until colours swam before his eyes. Nothing happened, and still he waited, braced for the attack that never came. And then, oh, reassuring sound, he heard the tear and crunch of an animal nibbling at the meadow grass!

His whole body relaxed, for the strain of anticipation had been very great. Fool that he was, to get windy like that, and just because one of the horses had moved across the field in his direction! The gypsies were rounding them up now, and more would be trotting over, gradually converging on their corner. As he waited there was a further soft pad of hooves on the grass, and a small pony nosed through the screen of blackness; advancing delicately, head outstretched, snuffling; a little suspicious of the twin sentinels standing silently in front of the gate.

Other dark forms loomed up, keeping their distance, and Crusoe looked across to Mr. Crawley, a few yards away on his left, wondering how best they could fulfil the gypsy's instructions and keep the herd together until he returned. What followed next, Crusoe had no idea.

A horse, somewhere over there, started suddenly; the plunge of hooves as it slewed round and trotted off was clearly noticeable. Mr. Crawley, Crusoe could just see, had turned away from him. He, too, was looking in that direction. All Crusoe's tense feeling returned. There *was* something wrong, he was sure of it! And yet, a minute passed and nothing happened, and gradually he relaxed again. But the same nagging, insistent voice inside him gave him no peace. After all, what right had Patch Cooper to be rounding up these horses? None, or he would have done it openly, and by daylight. If they *had* been followed (and why not, after all) then they must be prepared for trouble; serious trouble. And at that very moment, as if in answer to a low whistle that set all Crusoe's fears alive again, a black figure came flying over the gate just behind Mr. Crawley. The creak and tiny rattle of the chain; the thud of feet as the vaulter landed in the field, seemed huge sounds, close to them. Crusoe opened his mouth to shout a warning, but his throat contracted and for a brief instant he could not move. Everything happened so fast that he was given no time to recover himself. The man leapt into the field, running forward, his arm swinging up; but as the blow fell, Mr. Crawley turned and the knotted rope-end missed his head and glanced harmlessly off his shoulder. The two men were like jerking shadows; galvanized into sudden and completely silent activity on the edge of the dark field. Crusoe heard only the faint noise of the rope and then a

G

single, sharper sound; abrupt and instantaneous in its effect. Mr. Crawley, moving with surprising speed, drove his right fist full into his assailant's face. The man went down under the blow and stayed where he fell; sprawled and almost indistinguishable on the dusky grass of the meadow.

"Behind you!" Crusoe shouted, finding his voice at last. Another moment and he was grappling furiously as three more gypsies charged from the darkness; sending the horses plunging away in panic into the centre of the field. The newcomers, armed with sticks and the same, short lengths of rope, clearly had the advantage. Crusoe closed, taking the blows aimed at him on his body. He was a head taller than the two stocky men that went for him, but it was impossible to deal with them effectively, both at once. They pressed him slowly but surely towards the hedge, panting and cursing.

Suddenly—"Crusoe! Where are you!" called a familiar boy's voice. "This way, Michael! They're along here somewhere," and Titch was clambering over the gate, his brother close behind him. He peered into the dim field; saw the struggling figures, and hurled himself to the rescue.

"More of them coming," gasped Mr. Crawley, warding off a renewed attack. "I can't keep this up—much longer."

His hat gone and his collar and tie twisted and dishevelled, he was boxing with science and precision. His opponent had lost his stick and was vainly trying to force a clinch, but Mr. Crawley had so far kept him at bay with cleverly placed punches.

"All right, it's us," yelled Titch. "Get hold of his legs, Mike! Get round behind!"

Crusoe and the two gypsies were still tramping to and fro by the hedge.

"Patch Cooper's about somewhere," Crusoe managed to call to him. "Give him a shout!" He was half-smothered by his assailants; one of them had an arm round his neck and the other was grappling with his legs, trying to throw him off his balance. Crusoe felt himself giving way, they were swaying on the edge of the ditch; the hedge just behind them. With a crash, the three men, interlocked, came down together and rolled into the brambles, kicking and struggling, a tangle of legs and arms in the blackness.

Titch shouted in all good faith; there was an answering voice, and more shadowy figures came blundering into the scene of action. A torch waved; a thin beam of light probed here and there, revealing the situation, and with angry cries Levi Ayres and more of his cronies charged to the rescue of the gypsies. Mr. Crawley went down as the attackers swept through them, but Titch, dodging the blows aimed at him, managed to knock the torch from the holder's grasp and plunged the tiny area into confusion and darkness. This was their only hope, outnumbered as they were. And then, quite suddenly, they seemed to be surrounded by the huge shapes of snorting, nervously prancing horses; driven once again into this corner of the field by Patch Cooper and his followers, advancing in a steady ring behind them.

"Open the gate!" called a well-known voice. "Get the *grys* away!" and Titch, jumping across to unfasten the chain, was sent reeling backwards, his head ringing with the blow. Someone—he could make out a shadowy blurr—had stationed himself, stick in hand, by the entrance. What this fight was about, why Patch Cooper wanted the horses driven out of the field, Titch had not the slightest idea, and he hadn't stopped yet to think things over. Quickly, he slipped out of his jacket and holding it ready, ran in again towards the gate. The man struck out, Titch caught the blow on the soft folds of his coat, held up at the last moment before his face, and pressing home his advantage rammed his assailant against the bars of the gate.

"Quick!" he panted, as someone else ran up behind him. "Get the chain unfastened." But his head was jerked back; a sinewy arm wrapped about his throat. Titch kicked out like a mule; there was nothing else for him to do. The grasp relaxed; he tore himself free and retreated almost under the hooves of the advancing horses.

Looking up he caught a glimpse of a man mounted on a black pony, long legs dangling loosely, leading by a halter rope a gigantic horse that even in the dimness seemed to shine faintly pale, as if dappled with a sheen of moonlight. And there, before him suddenly, was a small figure fighting like a tiger; another backing him up —*Patch Cooper!* Titch slipped behind the horses; avoided the two pairs skirmishing like gamecocks, and the loop of loose chain fell with a rattle between his fingers as the gate swung wide.

The rider dug his heels into the pony, tugged at the halter rope; the horses swerved, and made for the dim opening. The fighters disengaged. One of the men made a violent leap at the pony's head and grasped the bridle. For a moment all was chaos in the gateway; rearing, terrified horses; shouting, furiously fighting men. The darkness was all movement, violence, noise. And then the rider on the black pony broke away, and with the great, pale horse beside him they thundered off; vanishing almost at once into the night. Slowly the echo of wild, unrestrained hooves pounding the grass faded into comparative stillness, broken only by the ceaseless, distant hum of music from the fair, and the night took a deep breath. But when Titch turned, prepared to renew the struggle, he found that Levi Ayres and his friends had disappeared; following in the wake of the vanished horses. Only one of the enemy remained and he was sitting, a little dazedly, on the grass, rubbing his head. Where were Crusoe and Michael? Was everyone all right? Titch retrieved his coat and groped around in search of the others.

Mr. Crawley was looking for his hat and nearly bumped into him. Crusoe, very much the worse for wear, was mopping his wounds with a handkerchief and exchanging a brief word or two with Patch Cooper and his friends. One of the gypsies was closing and fastening the gate against the escape of any more of the horses. But of Michael there was no sign. Titch called his brother's name aloud, but there came no reply. He called again, louder than before, and still there was no answer.

Crusoe kicked against the torch, dropped in the fighting, and finding that it still worked he shone the light around as they walked across the corner of the field. They did not have to search for long. Almost immediately they discovered Michael lying on his back, as if asleep on the grass, with a discoloured bump swelling on his forehead.

"Feeling better now?" asked Titch cheerily. They were all seated inside Patch Cooper's waggon. The kettle on the stove was singing and a large brown teapot stood warming beside it. The little gypsy was just about to make tea.

"Yes, thanks," said Michael, feeling his bump rather nervously with his fingers. "My head aches a little, still, but not so badly."

"You'll feel better than ever after a cup of tea!"

"I don't know what could have hit me," Michael confessed.

"You never will!" Titch reassured him. "It's a wonder we aren't all casualties. Enough sticks flying around!"

"They're a rough lot of fellows," said Patch Cooper, his beady eyes twinkling as he looked from one battered face to another. "Aye, brothers, you'll be carrying the marks on you for a few days yet!"

"Now then, Cooper!" Mr. Crawley retorted, "the kettle's boiling its head off, let's have our tea." He had recovered his old brisk manner and his face glowed a cheery red. One of his eyes was slowly darkening and looked odd and out of place on his precise countenance.

"I must say, you put up a tremendous show," said Crusoe admiringly. "I've not seen boxing like it since my college days."

Mr. Crawley flushed a deeper colour. "I haven't put on the gloves for years," he said. "But I was a keen boxer when I was your age, and one doesn't forget. Curious, really, how easily one slips back into these things."

Crusoe's hands, resting on the table, were scarred with scratches; his cheek and neck lined with vicious red marks. Not for nothing had he fought through the brambles in the ditch and under the hedge. "Now that we're cooled off and are all a bit straighter," he said, addressing Patch Cooper, "what about an explanation?

Don't you think it's time we knew what we were fighting about?"

"Some dirty piece of work, I'll be bound," said Mr. Crawley with a chuckle. "Come on, man! Out with it! We've supper ordered for eight o'clock up at the inn. Why, bless me . . ." He had opened his coat and pulled out a small gold watch. "Not far off that already."

"You don't want to be in any hurry, now you're here," said the little gypsy, pouring out mugs of strong, dark tea. "Levi and them fellows will be hanging around and you'll only run into more trouble. If you'd taken my advice you'd be sitting down now to a snug evening meal."

"Patch, we couldn't! We were bored stiff up there. And besides, I haven't made any inquiries yet about Derek and Diana. I think I'd better go along to Dareham and call at the police station. They'll be able to tell me if . . ." Crusoe had already risen from his seat.

"You don't want to move," said Patch Cooper very firmly. "Now you're here, you'll please stay here."

"But how long . . . ?"

"In half an hour," said the gypsy, pushing them their mugs, "I shall know whether or not Levi Ayres is going to hand over the money his wife stole."

"Were those his horses?"

Patch Cooper slowly nodded; his dark eyes steadily gazing at them as if daring them to expostulate or protest. Mr. Crawley seemed about to speak, but hesitated, and then closed his mouth. Nobody else said a word. They waited in the curious silence that was not stillness at all but steady, ceaseless, battering waves of sound vibrating, almost rocking the waggon on its springs; the drumming of wheels and the blare and trumpeting screams of the organs, as roundabouts, Dodg'em cars and switchbacks rumbled and thundered not thirty yards away.

"The big dappled grey, the percheron," Patch Cooper continued, "is Levi's waggon horse. He paid a lot o' money for that *gry* at Devizes spring fair a year ago."

"Then you're . . . you're holding the horse to ransom?" said Titch, gazing excitedly across the table. "What a stunning idea!"

Mr. Crawley tapped with his fingers and gave a little cough. Crusoe was looking down; he didn't want to catch the gypsy's eye.

"All wrong, you know," said the old gentleman at last, shaking his head. "Two blacks don't make a white. What happens if he refuses to pay? Goes to the police? We shall all appear in dock, I presume? The charge, horse-stealing!"

Michael stared, wide-eyed. Why, in olden times people were hung for that sort of thing! You'd be certain to be sent to prison, to-day. But Patch Cooper was smiling that crafty smile of his; his eyes black slits in his walnut face.

"If I know Levi, he'll get the money out of his wife," he said. "He's not going to risk his own skin. He'll keep out of the hands of the *Muskeros!*"

"Well, we shall soon see," said Mr. Crawley. "But I don't like it. I don't like it."

Titch was evidently the only person who was at all enthusiastic. "What have you done with the horses?" he asked, eager for more information. "When the chap rode off, where did he go?"

Patch Cooper pursed his lips. "Levi would give a lot to know *that!*" he said, and Titch did not press him any further.

They sipped their mugs of hot tea reflectively and a

G*

healthy colour began to ebb back into Michael's face
again. Outside the night was strident; vulgar with garish
light and blatant with a ceaseless, monotonous din. The
noise became wearisome; the tunes repeated themselves.
Music that had seemed gay and suitable enough when
they were in the thick of all the fun, became almost too
much to bear, shut away as they were now, inside a small
caravan. The clamour filled the night air; grumbled
outside the door, the walls, the window. And when the
door was suddenly opened the noise burst upon them like a
rush of water under heavy pressure. A lean, brown face
stared in; every line and wrinkle lit with the glow from
their lamp. His gaze met Patch Cooper's; he nodded
significantly and was gone. The door swung behind him
and muffled the orgy of sound. For a moment something
like quiet reigned inside the waggon. Then Patch Cooper
rose to his feet; very dignified; his beaky nose and small
stature suddenly of no importance, lost in this newly-
assumed air of grandeur.

"Mr. Crawley," he said, "the money will be paid over
to you in full to-night."

CHAPTER 17

"Gaol-Birds"

THE superintendent looked up from the papers on his desk. He removed his spectacles and surveyed the group before him; the two children with frightened, tired faces, dwarfed by the vast bulk of the policeman who had brought them in.

"But, constable," he said, "did you take any steps whatever to search for this gentleman—this Mr. Robinson?"

"No, sir," replied the policeman, impassive as ever. "I brought them straight along to the station, as I assumed was my duty, sir." His voice, respectful though it was, contained a hidden rebuke. The superintendent tapped his glasses gently on the desk.

"On another such occasion, constable," he said, a little wearily, "you will endeavour to introduce an element of common sense into your conception of 'duty.' You have a description of the gentleman we want. I would like you to return to the fair and look around for him. I think, in view of what we have just heard, there is a chance he may be there. Certainly it is a possibility to explore. I shall expect you to report back in an hour's time. You can leave the children here with me."

"Very good, sir." The policeman swung majestically on his heel. His expression left no doubt as to his disapproval, but orders were orders. The superintendent sighed with relief when the door swung behind him and became suddenly very human.

"I'm sorry about this," he said, leaning forward in his chair and talking quietly, confidentially. "But if your

friend's still around where you saw him, Williams will
soon bring him along."

Diana could have cried again; with relief this time.
Here was someone who believed them; who actually
believed they *had* seen Crusoe. But the superintendent
was still talking.

"I'm afraid my room's not the lap of luxury," he said
smiling, "but there's a fire to sit by and you'll find chairs
over in the corner. Take off your coats and put your
luggage down by the door. I want you to make yourselves
at home. I expect you're hungry. You must have done
some travelling to-day."

Derek tried not to nod too vigorously.

"I'll see what we can provide." A small bell on the
desk top was pushed twice and a young man—in uniform
—answered almost at once. Like everybody else here, he
looked curiously incomplete without a helmet or any
sort of a hat at all. Uniforms didn't seem to go with
bare heads, Diana thought to herself.

"I have visitors, Tomkins," said the superintendent
pleasantly, and the tall young man did his best to conceal
his surprise. "Can you manage us a pot of tea for two—
no, let's have three cups. I'll have one myself. And what
about cake?" The young man shook his head with evident
regret. "No cake. That's a pity. Hot toast instead, then.
Wait a moment! Perhaps our visitors would care to
make their own toast at the fire, here? Glorious occupa-
tion!" The young man's eyebrows shot up; clearly he
had never seen his chief in such a festive mood before.
"We own a toasting-fork, I think, Tomkins? Good, bring
it along then. Our appetites are thoroughly roused, so
you won't keep us waiting, will you?"

The young man called Tomkins retired precipitately,

and in less than ten minutes Derek and Diana were
sitting in front of a fine coal fire, toasting themselves,
and large slices off the white loaf, all at the same time.
The smell filled the room, but the superintendent,
scratching away busily with his pen or answering the
telephone, worked on as if nothing was happening; his
own cup of tea at his elbow.

"This is what happened to Mr. Toad," whispered
Diana, her teeth meeting in the soft, luscious, thickly-
buttered toast, "when *he* went to prison."

"We're not in a dungeon," Derek objected. "I don't
call this even being in prison."

"I wonder if they keep prisoners here," whispered
Diana in an awed voice.

"Not a single one, just at present," said the superintendent cheerfully. He had overheard her remark.
"Most law-abiding town, this. Makes us fellows lazy!
Would you care to inspect the cells after you've finished
your tea?"

"Yes, *please!*" Derek exclaimed eagerly, but Diana, as
decidedly, shook her head.

"Now I know what *you're* expecting to see!" said the
superintendent, looking across at her, his eyes twinkling.
"Slimy, green walls and dark, damp dungeons; rusty
chains; all that sort of thing! Aren't you?"

Diana held her slice of toast in her fingers; her mouth
half-open; her expression frozen in horror. "Well, not
quite . . ." she managed to gulp breathlessly.

"Excellent education for you both to have a look
round," decided the superintendent. "No sign of
Williams yet so we've time enough. I'll take you around
myself."

Very reluctantly Diana allowed herself to be led along

a clean, well-lit corridor; down stone steps; through heavy iron doors, painted an even grey.

"Mind you," said their guide, "this is a modern building, and not all police stations are as good. But this is what they all should be like."

They entered a long, narrow passage, lined on one side with a row of doors; each with a centre grille. With the same bunch of small keys he carried the superintendent unlocked one of these doors and pushed it open, switching on the light. Nervously Diana followed Derek inside. A sudden thought struck her. This might be a ruse; a trick on his part to shut them up down here! She half-expected, for the briefest of moments, to hear the clang of the iron lock as the thick, heavy door shut behind them. But instead she heard the superintendent's cheerful voice as he pointed out, with justifiable pride, the amenities of this, the first and (most emphatically, if she could help it) the last prison cell she was ever likely to visit.

They stared curiously round the little, bare, white-washed room. Everything was spotlessly clean and dry; two large, silvered hotwater pipes ran across at the foot of the far wall and the cell was almost too warm and stuffy for comfort. There was a window; a black oblong, high up, and strongly barred. The centre light threw no shadows; everything was evenly lit. The bed was a wooden shelf that could fold back against the wall. There was one chair, and a small mat on the concrete floor; other than these, the cell was empty of furnishings. So clean and dry was everything, there seemed no chance at all of a mouse or even a spider for the prisoner to make friends with. Perhaps there was something to be said for the "bad old days" after all. But they often had to put up with snails and rats and things, too! Diana shivered, and decided that cement and whitewash and central heating was by far the best idea.

They clattered up the flight of stone steps again and emerged in the hallway by the large, glass entrance. Two people were at that moment pushing through the door. First came the large, burly, blue-clad figure of Police-Constable Williams, and after him a tall thin man, tweed coated, his fair hair rumpled; face showing badly scarred in the bright light. Derek and Diana rushed towards him, shouting their eager welcome. *Crusoe! Crusoe at last!*

"But your face!" Diana exclaimed a few moments later, after the first excitement had died down. "You're scratched all over!"

Crusoe, conscious of the gaze of the superintendent and constable, rubbed his cheek with his fingers.

"Ran into some brambles," he said, half apologetically. "Bird's nesting."

A cheerful party was gathered round the trestle table at the inn. The room papered with pig prizes looked much more homely and pleasant than before; the curtains drawn; lamp glowing on the table; a fire crackling in the grate. The cloth was spread, the meal eaten, and empty plates and glasses were strewn before them. Derek and Diana, recovering from their first surprise at meeting Mr. Crawley once again, discovered that he had known them to be imposters right from the very start, but had said nothing; amused to see how Mrs. Potts and Cynthia handled the affair between them. They learnt why Crusoe and the others were here and

heard the night's work discussed in brief undertones. No
further word yet from Patch Cooper or one of his
minions. Mr. Crawley, glancing at his watch, doubted if,
after all, he would be paid to-night. They had left the
little gypsy's waggon some good while ago, soon after he
had announced the success of his venture, and had been
escorted as far as the entrance gate of the fair. At that
point the large figure of a constable stepped from the
side of a stall, where he had been standing like some
imposing statue, watching the crowd pass, and for a
moment they had been very unpleasantly surprised
indeed. All was up, then; the game had been discovered?
But the constable's first words reassured them, and Crusoe,
greatly relieved, had walked with him to the police
station to recover his long lost charges, while the others
made their way up the hill again to the inn above the
town.

They had found supper waiting for them, and the
landlord hid his surprise as best he could at the sight of
their battle-scarred faces. He contented himself by
asking, with heavy sarcasm, if they had enjoyed themselves at the fair. He got no change out of Mr. Crawley,
who assured him that they had had a thoroughly good
time and were quite ready for a meal! Crusoe, Derek
and Diana joining them, they sat down in the same
little room where they had waited all those weary hours.
Michael, who had fully recovered his spirits, wanted to
demonstrate the barrel organ there and then, but was
firmly kept in place by his elders.

As they sat round the table, the lamp standing in the
centre, Derek could scarcely stop looking at them all. He
was fascinated by Mr. Crawley's black eye, which was
now ripening to a very fine shade of plum. Michael, too,

looked awful with that great yellow-green bruise on the side of his forehead; and Crusoe might have been tattooed, the criss-cross scarlet threads ran so evenly across his cheeks. Titch seemed to have come off best, but he could have shown them a fine lump on his head, hidden by his hair. What a fight they must have had! Fancy Michael, too, being in the thick of it; he was no older than they were. And they had found him, afterwards, lying unconscious on the field! A real casualty! Derek looked at him with greatly increased respect.

They had had to describe their own adventures, needless to say, and they added up to a goodly sum, all told. Derek and Diana, as they recounted their story, often wondered if, really and truly, so much could have happened to *them*. One thing after another, in rapid succession; they could hardly believe it was true! And what a stroke of luck, that they should have seen Crusoe at the fair, just for a brief moment as he fled between the tents. Otherwise they would never have been here at all.

Supper over, Mr. Crawley pushed back his plate and made as if to rise. "I think I'll just make sure the pony's bedded down comfortably," he said. "Always better to see for oneself."

"I'll go for you," Titch volunteered, "I know the way to the stables."

Mr. Crawley was quite glad to remain seated by the fire. "I've had my share of exercise this evening," he admitted, yawning and stretching his legs out to the blaze.

Titch was back in a few minutes, his face strangely excited. He sat down and glanced around the room before speaking.

"Pony all right?" asked Mr. Crawley.

Titch nodded, hesitating before he spoke. "The grey's in there, too," he said at last, "or else a horse exactly like it. And I saw a man waiting in the shadow outside —at least, I'm sure it was someone. He slipped away as I came out of the house." He sounded quite bewildered. The effect of his news on the party round the fire was immediate. Mr. Crawley slapped his knee.

"The rascal!" he muttered, only half seriously. "So *this* is his hideout, eh? No wonder he wanted us to stay put and keep our noses indoors! And what happens now, eh? What's the next stage in the game?"

No-one answered. Instead the silence of the room was broken by the sound of trotting hooves; the roll of wheels on the road outside. The cart came closer and stopped by the inn doorway. As one man, the party at the table rose and went to the window. Dimly, for the pane of glass reflected the light of the lamp, the flickering red of the fire, they saw two people climb from the small trap and make the pony fast to one of the posts of the fence. As the newcomers turned to enter, the curtain was let fall again and they retreated into the room.

"I wonder . . ." Mr. Crawley was heard to murmur, as they waited, listening intently.

The confused murmur of voices in the tap-room across the passage grew suddenly louder. The strangers, whoever they were, must have joined the villagers in that smoky, crowded little room with the dartboard and the table skittles. But the door remained open a long time and then the landlord's voice was to be heard in the passage and somebody thumped on their own door.

"Come in!" said Mr. Crawley, and the landlord's red face poked through the opening, his large body remaining outside.

"Two persons to see you, sir," he explained in his hoarse voice.

He bobbed out of sight as the two men followed each other into the room. The first was a lean, cadaverous figure, whose clothes might have been folded twice round his bent, hazel stick of a body. His sallow, wrinkled face was strangely familiar. Crusoe was the first to recognize him as the gypsy who had stared into Patch Cooper's waggon, with never a word, to deliver the good news. And behind him, more than a little contemptuous of the whole affair, swaggered Levi Ayres himself; a gay necktie fastened round his throat with a large gold pin, shaped into a horse's head. His black, beautifully oiled hair shone under a brand new cap. If anyone ever looked prosperous, he did, and the two men afforded the most painful contrast. Patch Cooper's friend might have been a beggar, and a badly-off, unsuccessful beggar at that!

But Titch, from his seat on the far side of the table, saw that his late adversary had not escaped from the fight without a blemish. Levi Ayres, like Mr. Crawley, had carried away with him a souvenir of the evening's contest upon his swarthy, unpleasant-looking face.

"Well, gentlemen, well met," he began in a loud voice, shouldering the thin man to one side and advancing to the table. "I think we have a small account to settle, eh, Mr. Crawley." He bent and stared maliciously at the company, but in view of his own scarred face his triumph was hardly what he could have desired. "Now let me tell you straight, all of you—you're luckier than what you deserve to be! I'm not a man to be made a fool of! You owe a lot to me. I'm paying over, but I'm not beat, see? I don't want your old woman's dirty bit o' money, Mr. Crawley. I got more money than I can do with, an' that's a fact. You can have your sixty quid, but I ain't forced to pay. Oh, no! You're lucky, you are. I could a' got the lot o' you into trouble over to-night's work, *and* you know it."

Mr. Crawley ignored Levi Ayres and turned to the thin gypsy, who was standing, silent and motionless, with folded arms.

"Will you please see that the money is paid over without further delay," he said.

Levi's face darkened. "Eager for your money, Mr. Crawley?" His eyes in the lamplight gleamed with anger. He plunged a hand inside his coat and pulled out a thick bundle of notes, tied like a parcel with a piece of string. "You'd rob a gypsy, would you? Where's your pride, *gorgio!*" As he spat out the word, he flung the money down on the table in front of Mr. Crawley. Diana jumped, she just couldn't help it, and Derek, Michael, Titch and Crusoe stared at the old gentleman, wondering what was going to happen next.

Mr. Crawley made no move for a moment. Then, slowly, indicating the notes before him, he demanded a count.

Levi's face, dark before, went black with fury. He stormed and raved; strode to the door and opened it; returned to shout more oaths and swear that never would he touch the filthy money with his hands again. But the quiet, iron will of Mr. Crawley gradually dominated him. Gradually the logic of the bald statement —no horse until the money was counted and the sum found to be correct—sank home, and his bellowings became vicious protestations, changing at last to the whine of a man who accepts defeat. If only he had known! thought Titch. If he had seen what he had just seen, and knew how near he was to the great, grey horse! But Levi Ayres had been brought out in the trap by a roundabout route, and every precaution had been taken that none of his followers should know where he had gone, or be able to trace his whereabouts.

And so, as they sat round in the lamplight, they watched his brown fingers slip the string from the tight wad of notes and slap them, one by one, on to the table. Never before had they seen such a lot of money. Ten, twenty, thirty . . . the pile grew and still the monotonous voice counted, and they all repeated the numbers silently to themselves, keeping check on the mounting figure. *Fifty-seven, fifty-eight, fifty-nine and sixty!* The last note was banged down on the untidy, scattered heap and—"I hopes you're satisfied, Mr. Crawley!" snarled the disgruntled Levi Ayres.

A few minutes later they were all watching at the window and saw the pony and cart drive off with three men hunched on the seat; while behind the trap, fastened by a rope to his halter, trotted the huge, pale moonlight-coloured horse, majestic and magnificent; the sharp clomp of his hooves belying his ghostly appearance as he melted into the darkness under the scattered stars.

"I wonder what the gypsy said when he found he was here!" said Michael thoughtfully.

CHAPTER 18

Hands Round the Oak

DRAGGING a large, dead bough behind him, Titch passed from the patterned shadow of the trees into the full sunlight of an open glade. He heard the sound of distant voices, the chop, chop of a hatchet, and a faint blue swirl of smoke drifted through the branches. The forest was beginning to show a green mist of opening buds where only browny-gold twigs had laced themselves, a few days earlier, against the blue and white of a cloud-chequered sky. A deeper green carpet, studded with flowers, spread away between the trunks, and moss-covered roots ran everywhere, like living veins. The trees arched gracefully; rising, bending, curving back and over; frozen into a swaying, stately dance. The breeze moved only the slenderest branches; only the tips of their fingers. Farther away, the stockier, thickset trunks of older trees stood, foursquare, rigid; as unmoved as blocks of granite. And yet even their buds were ripe and ready to burst, green winged, into summer foliage. Beneath their hard, wrinkled bark the sap had risen, spreading to the outermost twigs. They looked asleep, those hoary old stumps!—when they were as awake and alive and as aware of the warm sun as the tiniest plant that opened a flower, sheltered in a hollow between their outstretched roots.

Titch plodded on towards the camp, recognizing the various sounds from far off; hearing someone singing in a high, clear voice. That was Crusoe chopping wood for the fire; Diana probably, and Michael, rattling the cooking things; Derek shouting at them from over by the stream, where he was fetching water for Prince. And that was Cynthia, of course, singing. Titch grinned as he thought of her—a fiery little spark if there ever was one! She never should have been a cripple! It was amazing, really, how much she managed to do. She was enjoying every minute of this holiday, and living it all over again every evening, in the caravan. So Diana had said. She simply wouldn't stop talking and go to sleep. This was the most wonderful thing that had ever happened to her—but then, what sort of a life *did* you lead, if you couldn't use your legs? Diana had fought tooth and nail to bring her along with them; Titch admired her for that. She had persuaded Crusoe; broached the matter with Mr. Crawley; even tackled the redoubtable Mrs. Potts herself—and this had been by far the most difficult task of all! Never before had Cynthia been out of her Potty's sight. To let her go off camping—*camping*—with strangers, in a caravan; why, she'd never survive, the poor pet; it would be murder; sheer murder, for such a delicate child! The only possible solution to the problem was that she, Mrs. Potts, must come along too, to look after her mite, since Cynthia had so obviously set her heart upon the holiday. At that, Crusoe, Titch and Derek had dug in their heels, and even Diana felt this to be rather much of a good thing. Besides, there was only room for one extra; Cynthia could sleep with Diana in the caravan, while the others camped out in tents. So ran the ultimatum, and rather to their surprise Mr. Crawley had accepted and overruled the anxious forebodings of Mrs. Potts.

That was all four days ago, soon after they had returned from their chase after the gypsies. They had slept the

night at the little inn on the hilltop, wondering, rather
anxiously, if Levi Ayres and his followers would return to
try and obtain the money by force. But the morning
dawned, nothing had happened, and they were soon
making their way back again into the forest. Lunch-
time saw them at the Crawley's house, and Mrs. Potts'
relief at their return was unbounded; to say nothing of
Cynthia's welcome! But their faces! Mr. Crawley's black
eye nearly occasioned another fit of hysterics. The medi-
cine cupboard in the bathroom was turned inside out;
bottles and jars by the armful were brought down and
their varied contents so liberally applied that the house
soon smelt like a chemist's shop! They had bad news for
them, she said—possibly not so bad after all, Mrs. Potts
hinted, with a sly glance at Cynthia. Cousins Philip and
Margaret had left that very morning. They had done
nothing but quarrel since they came; declared the
country to be as dull as ditchwater; complained that the
nearest cinema was impossibly far away and, after renewed ructions, had packed and left for their home in
London. "Nothing to *do*, here," they had declared.
"Nothing ever happens in the country."

Phew! Titch remembered their expressions when they
heard that one, and chuckled again, tugging at his
great bough that had jammed behind a tree trunk.
Cynthia was well quit of *them*, and now she and Diana
were as thick as thieves, and this holiday was doing her
a world of good. At first she had wanted to be lifted and
carried about everywhere, like a child; because, of course,
they had not been able to bring along her wheeled chair.
Now she welcomed her irons and crutches, and went
everywhere with them; tried her level best to do everything they did. She even tried to bring in firewood and

carry the jug of water! She had pluck enough for a thousand, Titch decided.

Titch had, as a matter of fact, assumed a distant, but very watchful, guardianship over the crippled girl. Diana was her chief companion, but she was not always strong enough to pick her up, or carry her over an awkward ditch, or surmount some tangled barrier on one of their walks. But Titch was always on the spot and ready to help. He used to joke with her, tease her until her pale, rather wan face, shone pink and her eyes sparkled with mingled fury and laughter. He was always encouraging her to try and do more, to attempt this or that new feat, and Cynthia responded so actively that even in the few days she had been with them she seemed to have doubled her strength.

"That Potts woman was doing her no good," Titch had confided to Crusoe one evening. "From what Diana said, she was always damping her down and treating her like a bit of cracked china. She'll never get strong if she's wrapped up in cotton wool." And to test out his theory he took Cynthia climbing trees; only low, easy ones, it's true, with plenty of branches right down to the ground. But as he lifted her gradually higher, holding her fast, he seemed to be infusing some of the spirit of his own healthy, well-developed body into her thin frailty, and the stifled current of her life began to flow in a more normal way.

"For goodness sake, don't overdo it," Crusoe warned him, aware of the responsibility that rested with them. "Don't rush her! You're like a bullock with a kitten, and you'll wear her out." And Titch had promised to be steadiness itself.

As he approached the camp site, he saw the caravan

between the trees, and the smoke of the fire rising from the centre of a small clearing. Crusoe was still plying his axe and had already piled up a heap of small logs.

"You've been a time!" he called, looking across and seeing Titch. "Why d'you go so far away? Lots of wood around here."

"Not a piece this big," said Titch proudly. "Besides, I like looking about." He dragged the bough into the clearing; pausing to stare into the cooking pots on the way. "Lunch nearly ready?" he asked. "I'm surprised at myself, I'm so hungry. And how's the Prima Donna?"

But Cynthia had stopped singing. "Titch, d'you know what the D.'s have found?" she said excitedly. "We're quite near where they slept the night, and they've discovered the Royal Oak. They're going to take us there this afternoon."

"I'm sure this part of the forest is haunted," said Diana, turning a flushed face from the cooking fire. "We never thought we were anywhere *near* where— where we actually are," she finished lamely.

"That sounds Irish!" Crusoe paused in his work. "And doesn't say much for my map-reading!"

"Have you visited your hut again?" Titch asked.

Derek shook his head. "Not yet," he said, "but I'm sure we could find it, from the Royal Oak."

Diana smiled. "You know the way, do you? Are you *quite* sure?"

Derek stared at her, scenting a joke. "I'll see when I'm there!" he said.

Titch crossed to where Michael and Cynthia were sitting, leaning against one of the wheels of the caravan. "How are the tweet-tweets?" he inquired cheerfully.

Michael, brush in hand, scowled up at his large brother. His nature log book lay open across his knees.

"Go away, Titch!" said Cynthia. "Can't you see we're busy!"

"*We're!*" repeated Titch, sitting himself down comfortably. "And what's your job? Music while you work?"

"You wouldn't know, of course," said Michael loftily. "But all the really great painters always had assistants to squeeze out colours and wash their brushes and palettes and things."

Titch exploded. "I hope he pays you!" he exclaimed. "What d'you get? A lick of Chinese White every hour? D'you suck his brushes? I always did mine." He turned and saw that Crusoe had finished chopping. Titch never sat still for very long at a time. He was on his feet again in a moment and taking the axe, began work on the huge branch he had brought into the camp.

"I thought I'd leave you to deal with that!" said Crusoe, watching the splinters fly. "I'll lend a hand with lunch."

"And afterwards," said Diana, unbending from the fire and speaking seriously, like someone giving a toast, "the Royal Oak!"

"The true, if not the one and only, Royal Oak!" Crusoe repeated, quite as seriously, and then added, in a lighter tone, "I'm still kicking myself for leading you astray, like that. Comes of being too economical over telegrams!"

Two hours later the forest was bathed in the softer, golden light of mid-afternoon. Strung out through the trees, Crusoe and Derek ahead; Michael and Diana, with Cynthia swinging along on her crutches, close behind them; Titch, whistling merrily, bringing up the rear; they left their camping ground and made their way through the trees towards the largest, and possibly the oldest, tree of all.

"We must try and find the plantations again," said Diana. "We were looking for them last time we were here, and that was how we got lost. I wonder if we'd get lost a second time?"

"I can't believe you were really all by yourselves in the forest, all night," said Cynthia. "Weren't you terrified?"

Diana tried to remember. "No, mostly uncomfortable," she decided at last. "You see, we knew we were the only people, and there was nothing else to be afraid of."

"You spent ages hunting for Crusoe, didn't you?" said Michael. "I bet you were annoyed when you got to the oak and didn't find him."

"I was, rather, but Derek was expecting it, I think," said Diana. "He was so sure Crusoe had gone off with you and the gypsies. All because of Titch's penknife."

"He was glad to get that back," said Michael. "Weren't you, Titch?"

"What?" said the rearguard, breaking off his whistle. He trotted a few steps and caught them up. "Oh, yes, my knife." He fished in his pocket and handed it across.

"I don't want it. I was saying you were glad to get it back," explained Michael.

"I should say so! Look at that blade." Titch opened the penknife and showed the large blade worn thin by continual sharpening. "Like a razor," he said. "Cut anything."

"How near are we to the oak?" Cynthia wanted to know.

"Getting tired already!" Titch exclaimed. "We haven't got things to help us along, like you have, and *we* aren't complaining!"

Diana and Michael joined Cynthia in shouting him down. "Not far, honestly," said Diana. "Not more than another five minutes. But have a rest now if you'd like. Don't take any notice of Titch."

Cynthia decided she could stick it and earned Titch's ironic congratulations.

"You wait till you break your ankle or something," she flashed across at him. "You'll have to hobble along on a stick, and I shall go miles farther than you, then."

"I twisted my ankle about a week ago," Michael told her. "When we first came down here. I still feel it sometimes."

"I don't mind about *you*. Doesn't *he* ever have anything the matter with him?" Cynthia indicated the cheerfully grinning Titch.

"Royal Oak ahead!" cried Derek, and they pressed on, to stand at last at the foot of the enormous trunk. The sun had gone behind a cloud and for a moment the forest was darker and more sombre than before, with no golden light and interlacing shadows to relieve the grey, repeating pattern of the trees. And here in front of them, black and gigantic, was the tree that dwarfed all others; the true centre, the hub of all the forest. They gazed up at the massive branches; the great arms shooting out abruptly from the central pillar. Even Derek and Diana were impressed, seeing the oak for a second time. Certainly, it had grown no smaller.

"We came from over there," Diana murmured to herself. "And went back more that way. If we were to take the path by those holly-trees, we might reach the bridge and the stream and the bracken hut."

She remembered the cold feel of the water on her lips; the wet touch of the ends of her hair on her neck when she stood up again, climbing the soft bank. Something had splashed in the blackness under the brick arch. And then the night, the dreadful night, that had started quite comfortably; she and Derek talking together, each smothered in a pile of tickly bracken. The endless wait (shivering, stiff, aching all over) for the dawn to break; the night dragging itself out, minute by minute, to an eternity of cold darkness, until it seemed impossible that the sun should *ever* rise again. How clearly it all came back! The walk through the damp mistiness of the very early morning they had welcomed by contrast, and exercise soon warmed them up and things had looked a great deal more cheerful. Once out on the road (and how they had found their way through the forest neither of them knew for certain) they were swept up in an astonishing whirl of movement. From that lift in the milk lorry, through the noisy and altogether unbelievable breakfast at *Freddies*, with the crowd of drivers standing around them; on down to Littleport in the fourteen-wheeler, and on from there in an amazing number of different vehicles; post vans; private cars; cattle trucks; one person handing them on to another; they had gradually worked their way nearer to the fair.

At first no-one knew for certain where it was. They thought this, they believed that. Then they had passed through villages with old posters still adhering to the tarred walls of barns. The fair had gone through here, but how far had it travelled since then? Nobody knew for certain until, late in the afternoon, they found a man who could tell them what they wanted to know. Dareham was the place; to Dareham they must go! No railway, no main road. They had to strike across country and lifts were few and far between, and mostly short at that.

Farmers returning from market, a red G.P.O. van collecting letters from the village boxes. Darkness had fallen again before they reached the town, and the gaily coloured archway of lights welcomed them to the fairground. And, as a final blow, had followed their arrest by the dolt and dunderhead of a policeman just at the very critical moment! What a time they had had!

Diana blinked and came back to the forest again. Crusoe was calling to them all to form a ring round the base of the great tree, standing with their faces to the rough bark and linking hands.

"It's a tremendous size," he was saying. "Must be twenty feet or more. Come on, Diana, let's see if we can join up."

"The *Guide Book* says . . ." Derek was spread-eagled, arms outstretched, between Crusoe and Titch. He tried to remember what the girth measurements were. The caption to the photograph gave all the details, but he had forgotten the figure, and the book was back at the camp. Nobody minded, however, as nobody was paying him any attention.

They had all joined hands, now; all but Cynthia, who stood a little way off, supported on her crutches. She was watching them eagerly, her pale face with its frame of untidy red curls no longer wistful, but glowing and obviously happy. Crusoe held Derek's hand, Derek linked Titch, Titch held Michael and Michael grasped Diana's left hand. But there was still a large gap, though they strained and flattened themselves against the deeply scarred bark. Crusoe's fingers and Diana's fingers groped unavailingly. Though they could not see, there was at least four feet of the trunk between them.

"Come on, Cynthia!" they called. "You're needed. We want you! Come and complete the circle!"

"Just think how long this tree has stood here," said Crusoe, staring at the gigantic branch high above his head. "This must have been a large tree when the Armada sailed up the channel. I expect most of its fellows were cut down, then, to build our ships. And who can tell—it may be standing here long after we've all gone. What a life! Hundreds and hundreds of years."

Cynthia, swinging across in answer to their summons, had balanced herself between them, and carefully steadying her crutches, held out her arms. Her hands reached and grasped Diana's and Crusoe's, and the Royal Oak was spanned.

"Hundreds of years," she repeated softly. "Standing in the same place!" And Cynthia, the cripple, shook her head. "What would be the good of living at all?"

Leaning back as far as she dared she gazed up the towering pillar of creviced bark, and followed the arm of the bough as it shot out and up again, dizzily high; branching, dividing, growing smaller, until, like thin fingers, the branches became twigs and the twigs, blunt-ended, prodded their black buds into the cloudy April sky.

THE END

What is the title (you may ask) of David Severn's

NEXT BOOK?

We don't know!

But he is planning another story with new characters, a different family and further exciting adventures, and it will be published by

JOHN LANE THE BODLEY HEAD LTD

To get it, ask your bookseller for the new David Severn